Dragon's Blood

On certain days, when the light falls just right, two hearts can find each other... even when they exist a century apart.

Dragon's Blood

SHADES OF TIME SERIES

TIME TRAVEL ROMANCE

KATHRYN KALEIGH

DRAGON'S BLOOD
PREVIEW: LAVENDER BLUE

Dragon's Blood

Prologue

REED SMITH

GRAY CLOUDS GATHERED on the horizon. A thunderhead interspersed with lightning.

And we were headed right into it.

I stared out the window, watching as we passed over the treetops. A river. A few cottages.

Normally we wouldn't fly into a storm like this. It was certainly not in our best interests.

But we had gotten the call to rescue a squadron of soldiers that had taken enemy fire.

There was wounded. They needed us. Air Force Pararescue.

Today it was just me and my buddy. One pilot.

Six wounded. The number of wounded was always underestimated. Always.

"Prepare for turbulence," the pilot said over the speaker.

Not much we could do to prepare. My buddy, his name

was Jeff, glanced over at me. He'd been unusually quiet. Normally he was the chatty one. Jeff could talk about anything anytime.

"You alright, Jeff?" I asked.

"I'm good," he said, but looked away.

Something was bothering him.

I had no doubt about that.

I didn't know that this would be our last flight together.

CHAPTER 1
Reed Smith

Present Day

I STOOD on the street corner of Main Street and Alexander Avenue in the little mountain town of Whiskey Springs, Colorado and watched tourists crossing the streets like sheep. Families. Young couples. Older couples. A few people walking by themselves.

They followed the rules. For the most part.

Waited at the street corners for the green hand signals giving them the go ahead to cross the street.

The sun was warm on my head, bare except for my short dark brown hair, military haircut, but the breeze coming off the mountains had a chill to it. Even on a hot day in the middle of July, the heat was tempered by a coolness coming off the snowcapped mountains.

I stood in place, like a statue at attention. I wore dark shades over my eyes. It felt odd to be out in public wearing blue jeans, a polo shirt, and white canvas sneakers. All new.

My feet glued to the sidewalk, I let people walk around me. It earned me more than a few curious and even more irritated glances.

The traffic lights turned red and the vehicles took their turn. Bumper to bumper. Tourists driving here and there. Into the national park for the day. Shopping. Some just driving through, out for a drive.

Then there were the locals. In a hurry to get where they were going. Mostly annoyed with the tourists, but most had sense enough not to show it. Without the tourists, the town would dry up into a ghost town.

Music blaring from one of the passing cars was followed by the loud beep of a horn.

It was funny. City people came out here to get away from the city, yet they brought the city with them. The sounds. The crowds. The impatience.

They didn't even realize it.

As the crossing light turned back to green, a couple of teenagers decided to break the rules and take a short cut. Dressed in shorts and brand new bright red Rocky Mountain National Park t-shirts, they headed across the street at a diagonal. Jaywalking.

The cop's shrill whistle stopped everyone in their tracks long enough to see that they weren't the ones in trouble.

Everyone except the two teens. They laughed and started running.

My muscles tensed with instinct to go after the two boys. But it was not my job.

Retired.

The word still felt gritty in my mouth.

Retired at thirty-two.

Four years of college—ROTC followed by ten years in the Air Force.

New President. New rules. New orders.

And just like that the military was done with me.

Honorable discharge and all that. Full benefits befitting the officer I was. Had been.

Didn't matter. My plan had been to be career military.

Just like my father.

But my father's purple heart had come posthumously.

I'd always known that no matter how hard I tried, I would never match my father's success. He had been a hero in my eyes.

But I'd always had a chance. As long as I was active military, there had been a chance. Now I was on the street. A civilian.

People walked around me through the next round of lights. More dirty looks.

The policeman stopped the two boys who had the decency to lower their gazes as he handed them a citation.

Good. Law and order at work.

I was a firm believer in law and order.

The boys had to learn early or they would never respect authority.

My father had taught me early and it had served me well.

Tired of getting dirty looks, I turned away from the intersection and ambled, hands in my pockets, down the sidewalk. Hands in the pockets seemed like breaking a rule. I did it intentionally. To try and blend in.

I passed a bookstore displaying the latest bestseller. Not too many people hitting the bookstore today. With all the digital books, I rarely saw anyone holding an actual paper book anymore.

I guess I was the exception. I liked the feel of a book in my hands. The turning of the page. The special bookmark my sister had given me as a Christmas gift. It was faded and tattered now, but I used it anyway.

I kept walking. Today I was not in the market for anything to read. I had a science fiction novel in my overnight bag.

The next shop was a ski shop. Empty. Not much business in the summer for a ski shop. Maybe they sold other things. I didn't stop in to see.

But I stopped at the next door. Considered. Then stepped inside.

Perfect.

It was half café. Half bar. The owner was smart, serving burgers and fries as well as beer and whiskey.

Cool. Dark. Quiet. The television over the bar broadcast a baseball game, but the volume was turned down to barely audible.

There were a dozen tables, half of them booths along the windows. The bar was on the back wall with a full mahogany top worn with age. Lots of dings, but still shiny. A large stone hearth fireplace, tall enough for a man to stand up in, was on the wall to the right.

Not empty, but not crowded.

Half a dozen people sitting here and there. A middle-aged couple sitting at a booth having a hamburger. The other customers sitting at the bar.

"Welcome to Whiskey Springs Saloon," the man behind the bar said. Slightly overweight, he sported a bushy beard and a full-neck tattoo.

"Thanks." I slid onto the nearest bar stool and tucked my shades into my collar. "Can I get a bottle of Mill—?"

The bartender slid a cold bottle of Miller Lite across the worn mahogany bar.

"Lite," I finished my sentence.

Odd coincidence. Maybe everyone ordered a Miller Lite.

"No problem," the bartender said. "Can I get you anything else?"

The bartender had a flat affect. No smile. No emotion. But he sounded friendly enough.

"I'll let you know," I said, lifting my bottle to him and taking a sip. The beer was icy cold. Just the way I liked it. My men had always ribbed me about my aversion to warm beer.

A man liked what he liked.

With a shrug, the bartender slung a white cloth over his shoulder and straightened the already perfectly spaced glasses hanging above the bar. Apparently not all the customers drank beer out of a bottle.

In fact, there was only one other fellow at the other end of the bar drinking beer. The others had glasses of what looked like whiskey.

Refusing to add it to my list of worries, I stretched out my legs and made myself comfortable.

I'd found my way here, presumably to think.

So think I would do.

My parents had brought me and my sister here every summer for a month-long vacation. A three-bedroom cabin on the river. As far as I could remember, it was always the same cabin. They must have had a standing reservation. It had only been one month out of the year, but it was the one constant in my life. We'd moved around a lot during the year as my father was stationed at one base, then another.

But every year we came back to this one little town. Until we didn't.

I was sixteen when it happened. My wounded father was flown to Germany and given the best medical care in the world. But he did not come home.

My mother and her two children stayed in Alabama where Father had left her. And we never returned to Colorado as a family. I had never come back either.

Until today.

A vacation spot should never be the one constant place in a child's life.

But in some odd way, this was home to me.

I ran my fingers along the smooth wood of the bar.

My life could turn now. Go in a completely different direction.

I'd never married or had children because I did not want to subject them to the military life I had grown up in.

But now...

I wasn't sure I was ready to do anything drastic.

I needed time to think.

To just be.

To get my bearings.

I did not have to hurry. The military was taking care of me, financially at least. I guess that was some consolation.

The grandfather clock standing next to the stairs leading to the second floor chimed the hour.

CHAPTER 2
Andrea Auclair

1866

I SAT at the vanity in my room and fussed with my hair.

I'd brushed it one hundred strokes just like my mother had taught me as a little girl. I might be twenty-one now, but it was one of those things that was ingrained in my system. Besides, most nights I found it soothing. Not tonight though.

Tonight I was nervous. I had no reason to be nervous. This was just a business deal. Not worthy of this level of worry. If this didn't work out, something else would.

I was just so weary of traveling. I wanted to just be somewhere. To be settled.

Breaking the silence, a horse and wagon traveled along the dirt road beneath my second-floor window. There was never much traffic in the small town. One of the things I liked about it.

Somewhere in the distance I heard a blacksmith's hammer banging against iron. Fashioning a horseshoe perhaps. So strange that horses wore shoes.

If I listened really hard, I could hear the strains of piano music drifting from the saloon. Someone was always playing the only piano in town.

A lot of the ladies here in town were from the south where learning to play the piano was a normal part of their upbringing. Just as it had been mine.

I had been in the saloon one time. Although it was overall what I had expected of a saloon in appearance, it felt more like a café with a bar in it. It had a wall of glass windows with a picturesque view of the Rocky Mountains.

Sitting here in my room, if I turned to my right, I could see the peaks of the mountains in the distance. It was full on summer and they still had snow on them.

Since I'd never seen snow, I could not fathom how snow could be there in the middle of summer.

Just one of the many wonders of this place I hoped to call home.

I wove a blue ribbon that matched my high-collared dress through my hair and tied it into a bow behind my ear.

Not exactly the look I was going for, but it would do.

The cook was downstairs, preparing supper. Even up

here, the scent of biscuits and gravy was strong enough to make my mouth water. We had not had much to eat on the long trip from New Orleans to Colorado. A lot of beans and stale biscuits. When there was meat, no one asked what kind it was. If we knew, it was doubtful we would have been able to eat it.

Twirling around on the bench, my clean muslin skirts rustling with the movement, I looked across the room at the supplies we had carted in the bottom of the wagon all the way from New Orleans. A stack of blank paint canvases tied together with a strand of rope. A box of paints and brushes and a box of charcoals.

It wasn't much to anyone else, but to my sister, it was of utmost importance.

I was certain Bailey was ready to spread them out somewhere and capture the wonderful things we were seeing. To do more than the few charcoal sketches she had done during our travels. But there had been so very much to do for the last few months.

It had taken all hands on deck. With me being the oldest of five children, each spaced one year apart, I had quickly learned to be even more responsible than I had been before.

When Father had gone off to fight in the war, he had left Mother in charge of their huge family. That had been five years ago.

Then mother had succumbed to a bout of yellow fever only a few months ago. I still felt like I was walking around in a fog. Still could not believe that both our parents were gone.

Next in line after our parents to take care of us was our uncle. Uncle Pete, never married, turned out to be not only a scoundrel, but also a gambler. He had gambled away our home. Fortunately, he had not had access to money in our parents' bank account, so I had that.

With my four younger siblings in tow, I had taken the money from the bank and the money our mother had squirreled away herself and essentially vanished into the night.

West.

Before the war, my father had often talked of going west. He knew nothing more of the west than what he learned from the dime novels he voraciously read, but it did not matter.

His dream had been passed on to me.

Not that it was my dream, necessarily, but maybe he had somehow made it my destiny.

Destiny was a slippery thing. Hard to hold, bouncing in what looked like a random fashion from place to place.

But I was certain it was far from random.

My father had shaped me. There was a reason he had told me stories of the west before I could even read. Planted those images in my head.

He had made me who I was. And my mother had made me responsible for my siblings.

Those two things swirled together inside me making me who I was.

So here we were. In the small town of Whiskey Springs, Colorado Territory.

With no idea of what would come next.

Whatever it was, I would handle it. My siblings and I had come this far. I told myself it would be an adventure.

Patting my cheeks and forcing a smile onto my lips, I prepared to face what surely must be the next chapter in our lives.

CHAPTER 3
Reed

MY THINKING WASN'T GETTING me anywhere, so I left some cash on the bar alongside my half-finished beer and stepped out onto the busy street. I walked a few steps, dodging the packs of tourists.

I squinted in the bright sunlight and automatically reached for my sunglasses. They weren't there. I didn't remember taking them off, but I must have left them on the bar.

I retraced my steps to the saloon.

Pushing the door open again, I stepped back inside the darkness.

Something was different.

It seemed darker, but that was to be expected with me coming in from the bright sunlight.

I couldn't see them, but I heard someone in one of the other rooms playing the piano.

I stood right there in the middle of the room and slowly looked around.

I had stepped into someone's parlor. There were no tables. No booths. There wasn't even a bar.

Instead, a roaring fire in the large fireplace provided a background for a sofa and two chairs. A crystal chandelier with a dozen flickering candles hung from the ceiling. All in all, it was a rather elegantly furnished room.

The tall grandfather clock was still there, steadily ticking away the minutes.

It was as though I had walked out and someone had completely changed the set.

But not only was this not a play, tables and people did not just vanish.

Somehow I had stepped through the wrong door.

The clock was still here.

I was about to turn and duck back out when a movement caught my attention.

Someone was coming down the stairs.

It was a young lady in full costume.

She wore a long blue floor-length dress with a bustle at the back. Strands of long brunette hair framed her face.

Smiling when she saw me, she looked like she had just stepped out of the pages of time.

Intrigued, I stood my ground and watched her.

"Good evening," she said, her voice laced with honey. She was southern. I'd say New Orleans.

"Good evening," I said. This was one of those rare times when I was grateful for my mobile childhood.

Keeping one hand on the rail and subtly manipulating her skirts with the other, she moved down the stairs. She appeared to be enviably practiced in her role.

She walked right up to me and held out a hand, palm down. A traditionally lady-like gesture. Not at all like a regular handshake.

"I'm Andrea Auclair," she said.

I took her hand and gave it a gentle squeeze.

Her eyes were a brilliant green framed by long, lush lashes. Her cheeks were flushed prettily. But it was her lips that stole my attention. Bow shaped and a deep subtle red. *Kissable.*

Even more amazing, she wasn't wearing a stitch of makeup. I was no expert, but I'd stake my life on that one.

All in all, she was an enchanting package. She looked like she was made for whatever role she was playing. Not a saloon girl. Her dress was too long and her neckline too high. A lady, I decided.

"Reed Smith," I said.

She looked at me quizzically, but swept a hand toward the sofa.

"Would you like to have a seat?" she asked.

Curious about this whole thing, I went along with it and took a seat on the sofa. She sat on the edge of the sofa, her back straight.

"Thank you for coming," she said.

I smiled. Role playing. Somehow I had stepped into some kind of role playing activity.

"I don't have a ticket," I said.

There was that quizzical expression again. "Neither do I," she said.

Alright, then. We'd settle up later. This was a far more interesting activity than walking up and down the streets watching tourists eating ice cream cones and getting busted for jaywalking.

"Can I get you some refreshment?" she asked.

"Maybe later," I said, not wanting her to leave my presence, even long enough to get us something to drink.

"Alright," she said. "How do you like Whiskey Springs?"

"I've always liked it," I said.

"Oh. You're from here then?"

"No. But I've been here before."

"Where are you from?"

I considered for a moment. I had used all sorts of answers before. But for some reason, I wanted to be truthful with this girl. Silly, I thought, since we were role playing.

"I'm not really from anywhere."

"Well, you have to be from somewhere," she said. "Everyone is from somewhere."

"I suppose you're right," I said, but not answering her. "You're from New Orleans?" It was more of a statement than a question.

"Of course," she said. "but you already knew that."

Now it was my turn to look at her quizzically.

"So what do you want to know?" she asked, toying with the silver locket around her neck and looking up at me from beneath those lush lashes.

I was military. I had been around. I knew about role play games.

But I had never walked into anything like this. Maybe this was some new kind of role play game they were doing in the private sector.

I glanced around. Definitely some kind of history oriented game suitable for the old west.

I could play along. Besides, I was not not more than a little intrigued.

Before I could answer, a middle-aged man of Chinese descent, dressed in a long white apron appeared at the door. He carried a tray with two crystal glasses and two decanters.

He set the tray on the coffee table in front of us and looked at Andrea.

"Is there anything else I can get for you?" he asked, with a smile.

"No, Hector," she said. "Thank you so much."

Hector nodded and left us.

So this was one of those games that involved other people. Very interactive.

I had the feeling I wasn't supposed to ask for the game's parameters. Either I was supposed to know already or perhaps there weren't any.

Andrea leaned forward. Filling my glass with amber liquid from one of the crystal pitchers, she handed it to me, careful not to touch my hand.

Then she filled her own glass from the other decanter.

"What brought you to Whiskey Springs?" I asked.

CHAPTER 4
Andrea

THE AIR WAS chilly and I regretted not bringing a shawl with me downstairs.

The fire in the fireplace kept most of the chill at bay, but I was too far away to reap much benefit from its heat.

Besides the crackle of the fire and the steady ticking of the grandfather clock, it was quiet in the house. My three sisters and my brother were out walking. They would be back soon and any semblance of quiet would be gone.

I needed to get this meeting over with before they came in.

I had not expected a man named Reed. I had, in fact, been expecting a man by the name of Alexander Avery. Dr. Avery, actually, the owner of this boarding house. But no doubt Dr. Avery was a busy man. I should not be surprised that he had sent someone else in his stead.

"Dr. Avery didn't tell you?" I asked, before taking a sip of my tea, hopefully to hide my annoyance.

He took a sip from his own glass. "I'm afraid not." His glance contained whiskey as opposed to mine that held tea. One of the first things I'd learned at Whiskey Springs was that ladies drank tea while men drank whiskey.

I was pretty sure it had started as a ploy to get men to spend more money in the saloons. The men buy ladies whiskeys without knowing those ladies were merely drinking tea. The more the men drank, the more money they seemed willing to spend.

Somehow this whole thing had transferred over into polite society.

"Very well," I said, cupping my glass of tea with both hands. "I suppose I shall have to start at the beginning then."

"I'm sorry for the inconvenience," he said.

He didn't look sorry. He looked... curious.

I took a deep breath and gave him the short version. It wasn't my fault that Dr. Avery had not properly prepared him for the meeting.

"My siblings and I recently arrived from New Orleans."

"Your siblings?" he asked with a quick glance around.

"They're walking outside," I said with a little wave of dismissal.

"I see."

Somehow I got the feeling he didn't believe me. Disregarding the feeling, I kept going.

"We'd like to rent this boardinghouse," I said. "Or perhaps even purchase it."

"Okay," he said.

I looked at him blankly. "Is there some kind of application?"

"Not that I'm aware of," he said. "you're here, aren't you? So it seems quite reasonable to me."

"Then you think Dr. Avery will say yes?"

"I should hope so."

I took another sip of my tea, then set the glass aside. "If not, we can go somewhere else," I said.

"I don't think that's necessary."

I glared at him.

"It almost seems like you want me to tell you no," he said.

I closed my eyes and shuddered. Before looking at him, really looking at him.

He was a handsome man with short hair. Clean shaven. He was, in fact, the cleanest man I had seen since before we left New Orleans.

He was wearing odd clothes, but things were different out here in the west and I was no longer shocked by much of anything. He looked a bit like he was smirking at me. I did not understand that. Yet at the same time, his deep sapphire blue eyes were locked onto mine. Those eyes alone were a little disconcerting.

"It's not that," I said. "I just didn't expect it to be this easy."

"Why not?"

"It's a long-term commitment," I said, though I really did not know how to answer him.

He smiled then, brightening his face. "Sometimes things just happen."

His smile, directed at me, sent little shivers up my spine —pleasant shivers.

"Yes," I agreed, leaning forward. Perhaps he was right. Perhaps this was fate. My mother had always said that when something was supposed to happen, it would happen smoothly. If not, there would be opposition. Perhaps this was a prime example.

"So," he said. "What do we do now?"

Before I could devise an answer, the door opened and my four siblings spilled in, bringing noise and disruption with them just as I had predicted.

"I suppose you get to meet my siblings," I said, standing up.

CHAPTER 5
Reed

FOUR ADDITIONAL PLAYERS walked into the room, bringing noise and chaos to what had been a quiet peaceful room merely seconds ago.

The three girls, dressed in long dresses similar to Andrea's, walked over to stand in front of the fire.

The one I decided was older than the other two whispered something to youngest sister and they giggled, reminding me of my own sister when she was a teen.

Apparently the Auclairs had managed to space their children out with an order to be envied by any commanding officer. I stood silently as Andrea introduced her siblings.

After Andrea, there were three other girls. Bailey, bright-eyed and rather seductive in the way she looked at me. Dakota, watching me with apparent suspicion, and the youngest, Elise with a happy-go-lucky air about her.

Then spaced right in the middle of the four girls, there

was Colton. I only knew this because Andrea introduced him as the middle child. It was apparently some kind of running joke among the girls. He was a handsomely lean young man with eyes that took in everything. I wondered how many times he had been required to come to the defense of his sisters.

Colton quickly excused himself and headed upstairs, no doubt happy to be away from so many sisters.

I would have questioned whether or not they were all really siblings, expect that they all resembled each other. The same dark brunette hair and bow-shaped lips in heart-shaped faces. Even Colton, personally, I would say was pretty.

After the quick introductions, Andrea stood and looked at me with something of a challenge in her gaze.

"So," she said. "now you see why we are in need of such a large house."

"I see," I said.

"Would you be so kind as to let Dr. Alexander know? I realize he sent you in his stead, but perhaps if you would put in a good word, then he will be more inclined to come to an amicable agreement."

"Of course," I said. "I will be more than honored to put in a good word for you."

"Thank you so much," she said. "Then if you'll excuse me, I have to make sure all of my siblings are fed and get them ready for bed."

It appeared to me that she was no older than her siblings, but for some reason she took responsibility for them.

She shot her sisters a warning glance when they giggled

again. It really didn't help. Girls would be girls. The middle girl had moved away from the others and stood watching me while she tugged off her gloves.

Andrea's eyes were a bright green with the most beautiful combination of shades of dark and light green shooting out from her pupils. I was mesmerized by her.

But she moved around me to the door and opened it.

"Good night," she said.

Then before I really knew what was happening, I was on the other side of the heavy wooden door. Back in the sunlight and thrust back among the tourists.

And I still did not have my sunshades.

Turning, I tried the door knob, but it was locked.

Well hell.

I knocked. Twice. But no one answered.

I know she had to hear me. She was just right there. It was just as bad as phoning someone who had just texted. You had to know they were holding their phone.

With no other option coming to mind, I went down the street to the general store to buy another pair of shades.

They didn't have the brand I liked, of course. I knew they wouldn't. Yet the markup on what they did have was about ten times what it should be. I knew these things from practically growing up here. It's why Mother rarely let us buy things in Whiskey Springs.

A tourist town, she'd say. And only tourists pay their exorbitant tourist prices. Today, though, I didn't care.

I just wanted my eyes protected.

I handed my new shades to the woman behind the counter.

"Have you heard anything about the new role-playing game two doors down?" I asked as I swiped my credit card.

The clerk, an older woman, lowered her glasses and looked at me like I'd just insulted her. "I don't get involved in such things," she said.

"It looks like some teenagers," I said. "being innovative. It's quite creative."

"No," she said. "I don't know anything about it."

"Do you think it's a thing for the tourists?" I asked, trying to go about it a different way.

"You're a tourist," she said accusingly.

Yep. Only a tourist would pay what I just paid for a pair of cheap sunglasses.

It was time to grab some dinner anyway, before finding my way to my cabin for the night.

Wearing my new sunshades, I stepped back out onto the sidewalk and checked my phone. No messages. No calls. No emails.

Such was the life of the newly retired.

A lifetime of dedication forgotten. Just like that.

My cabin was within walking distance of downtown. A touristy move, but it wasn't my fault the town had grown in the last seventeen years and I wanted to stay someplace vaguely familiar.

So I cut myself a break on that one.

But as I retraced my steps, I came to the door where Andrea Auclair had been.

Unable to resist, I turned the doorknob. It was still locked.

I stood there, puzzling over the whole thing.

I must have stood there for longer than I thought because one of the street cops stopped and glared at me from behind his own dark shades.

"Lost something?" he asked.

I looked at the officer. Chewing gum and looking at me like I was doing something wrong.

"I attended a role-playing activity here earlier and I just wanted to make sure I was paid up." It was rather lame, but it was the best I could do on short notice.

"Role-playing, huh?" the officer said.

"Yes. Some innovative teenagers."

"Do I need to ask what you and these teenagers were doing?" he asked.

I suppose that was his way of asking. "Talking," I said. I really did not want to get into trouble with the law. "Is it an old house or something?"

The cop, Officer Garrison, according to his name tag, stopped chewing his gum for about four seconds. "Tell me again why you care?"

"There were kids in there." I decided that taking a concerned tactic might be a better way to handle this. Whatever they were doing, it was apparently not something known about, much less condoned by the community.

"Shouldn't be," he said, chewing his gum again. "The building was condemned over a year ago."

Condemned. This could not be good. I glanced over at

the locked door, then down the street. There were no other doors like this one. It was the right door. I was certain of it.

"You look familiar," Officer Garrison said.

"My name is Reed Smith. My family visited here when I was growing up."

"Reed," he said. I saw it on his face the minute recognition hit him. "It's been awhile, but... I think we went hiking together."

"I'm sorry," I said, not feeling that same recognition vibe. That had been a long time ago. And I didn't remember any names. I did remember hiking with a local boy scout troop though. "Boy scouts?"

"Yes," he said, punching me good-naturedly on the upper arm. "I'm Brett Garrison."

"Brett," I said with a nod. It was enough for him to run with.

"Good seeing you, Buddy."

"You too," I said, going along with it, although had no memory of him. I'd been a lot of places since then. Met a lot of people. He, apparently, had not.

"Here." He took a step up to the door as he pulled a ring of keys out of his pocket. Keys jangling, he quickly found what he was looking for.

He put a key in the door lock, turned the knob, pushed the door open. Then he stepped aside so I could see.

I stepped up to the door and, removing my shades, looked inside. Nothing but a dark, empty space.

I looked at Brett.

"Go ahead," he said.

I stepped inside and placed my hands on my hips. Everything was gone. The huge fireplace was there, but it was cold and empty. There was no furniture. No grandfather clock.

The first time I was here, there was a bar. But no sign of that either.

"Was there a bar here?" I asked.

"It's next door."

"Right." So at least there was that explanation. And it was good to know I hadn't imagined the bar, especially since I could still taste the beer. But there was no sign of the Auclair family.

I stepped into the middle of the room. Even the windows were boarded up. There was absolutely no way this was the same place

"Thank you for letting me inside," I said, turning on my heels, nearly bumping into Brett. I had not realized he had followed me inside.

"Sure thing," Officer Brett said. "We'll get together. Have a beer one night."

"Sure thing," I said over my shoulder. Ready to leave now. More than ready. Then I stopped, turned around and held out a hand. "Good seeing you again." I had a feeling it was best to act like nothing was wrong.

Then I stepped back out into the crowd, dropping my shades back in place.

Reaching the intersection, I crossed the street without stopping. Fortunately the light was green. I kept walking, across two more intersections, down a gravel road, until I reached my cabin.

It was a simple little one room log cabin nestled against the rushing river bank. I walked around it to the edge of the river and sat on a boulder. Watched the water swirling around the rocks, rushing downstream. Watched a fish swimming near the surface in a little pool of water nestled in the rocks, coming to the surface, looking for something to eat.

But none of it registered with me more than in passing.

All I saw was Andrea Auclair sitting across from me. Looking at me with big, beautiful eyes. I had seen her. I had seen her brother and sisters come into the room.

They had been real. I'd stake my life on it.

Something was wrong. Very, very wrong.

CHAPTER 6
Andrea

I STIRRED at the mushy green peas in my plate. I'd sworn I'd never eat peas again after the war was over.

But here I was, a million miles across the country, and Hector, the boardinghouse cook had served up peas for us.

There were other things, too, of course. There were biscuits, always a staple, and a big slab of ham.

I should be grateful that my siblings and I had a hot meal to eat.

All four of my siblings appeared to be enjoying their supper as they chatted about what they had seen today and planning what they would do tomorrow.

We'd only been in Whiskey Springs a handful of days. Already, we all loved it here. But we were a big family and we needed lots of room. There was a total of six bedrooms upstairs.

Colton, being the only boy, had one of them, of course. I shared one with Dakota. Bailey and Elise shared a third.

If we could work out something so that we could have five rooms, we would not only have more space, but maybe Dr. Avery would reduce the price by letting us lease by the month instead of paying by the night, allowing us to stretch our money.

Until I found work, it was my job to make sure our money lasted, at least until my sisters were married. Colton could find work easy enough and I could manage on my own.

And even today, Bailey had come back from her walk with a pretty new hat. My siblings had never been deprived of anything, so saving money for a future they could not fathom was foreign to them.

I hated my role as protector of the money, and since I was only one year older than my next sibling down, it seemed more than a bit unfair that I was saddled with this role, but it fell to me nonetheless. Someone had to do it.

That, however, was not what had disturbed my appetite.

Reed and I had not finished our conversation when my siblings had come inside, causing commotion and chaos.

I had quickly ushered him out, not wanting him to think that we were too unruly to lease Dr. Avery's property.

I could understand how one would jump to that conclusion, just listening to the commotion they caused. I had not missed the way Bailey had looked at him from beneath her new bonnet. She was such a flirt. It would not pay for Reed to get the wrong idea. Heavens. Bailey would have him thinking we were here to open a brothel.

Bailey was the prettiest of us and she liked male attention. It would probably be a good idea to get her married off first. Before she could get into trouble.

At any rate, I had quickly changed my mind about sending Reed off without finishing our conversation and it had not been more than five seconds later when I opened the door I had just closed behind him. I had been thinking we could finish our discussion on the front porch. I had called out to Elise to grab my shawl from upstairs, then turned back to the open door facing the street.

There had been no sign of Reed. None. I looked right and left. I even walked to either side of the porch to look for him.

There was no way he could have walked away that quickly.

He had quite simply vanished.

"Someone is opening a dress shop," Elisa said. "They don't have much yet, but the owner said she could make Bailey a dress to match her hat."

Of course she did. Bailey, although a full three years older than Elise was already molding her younger sister in her likeness.

"Like Bailey needs another dress," Dakota said. Dakota, probably actually the prettiest of us all, but such a serious girl, she tended to be overshadowed by Bailey and Elise.

"We'll all get new dresses in good time," I said, weary of

such conversations. It would be so easy to pass dresses along from the oldest to the youngest of us, but it did not seem fair to me that just because someone was born a few years later, they should not get something new. If that was the case, then Elise would never get a new dress. The bad thing was that Elise really didn't seem to care one way or the other.

"Don't you need someplace to wear a new dress first?" Colton asked.

Colton was so much like me. Or at least like me without the peacekeeping part. He tended to just say what was on his mind.

He was right, of course. My sisters and I had more than ample clothes to wear and there wasn't likely to be any kind of special occasion out here where any of us would need a dress. A wedding for Bailey, though, would be a good occasion.

"Who was that man you were talking to?" Dakota asked, her brows creased in consternation. I'd told her she needed to stop frowning lest she get stuck that way. "He was not Dr. Avery."

"His name is Reed," I told her, stirring my peas. "Dr. Avery sent him."

"Did he agree for us to stay here?" Dakota persisted.

"Not yet," I said. "I think it's best if I talk with Dr. Avery himself."

"I agree," Dakota said. "He's the one who decides anyway, right?"

Dakota was far too old for her years.

I gave her a small smile. "I think so, yes."

"He was quite handsome," Bailey said.

I ignored Bailey's comment. It seemed I wasn't the only one who had noticed just how handsome the stranger was. But, unfortunately it did not seem to matter, since he had completely vanished.

CHAPTER 7
Reed

J US T AFTER ONE a.m. in the morning, I stood in front of
the vacant building. Unable to sleep, I had gotten up, pulled
on my clothes, and wandered back downtown.

The streets were empty this time of morning. Only the
occasional car passing by. Downtown looked like a ghost
town. It was strange, being in such stark contrast to the
crowds from daytime.

The bar, next door, however, was still open. Rock music
drifting from inside.

I tried the door. It was, of course, locked. Not wanting
to get arrested for breaking and entering, I went next door to
the bar.

The same bartender was there. The one with his neck
covered in tattoos. It made me cringe a bit, being from a
clean-cut military background. Guys in the service who had
tattoos had to keep them concealed at all times.

Only a handful of people were scattered around.

"Miller Lite?" he asked, sliding a bottle of beer across the bar.

"Sure." I took the beer, but didn't drink. Just held it in my hands.

I hadn't come for a drink. I was, actually, a bit obsessed with the building next door.

Since the bartender was hanging around, I decided to ask him.

"Do you know anything about the building next door?" I asked.

"The condemned boarding house?" he asked.

Boarding house. That made a bit of sense. "Yes."

"Been condemned for years. Sometimes people get inside. Homeless people. Mostly during the winter."

Homeless people. Andrea did not look homeless. And her siblings had just walked right in through the front door. Just as I had.

"What about other things?" I asked, reluctant now to talk outright about what I'd seen. "Like historical things?"

The bartender pulled out a cloth. Wiped at the bar in front of me. Leaned forward and, looking around, spoke softly.

"There's a legend around here," he said.

"A legend?" I felt a tingle down my spine. "What kind of legend?"

He shrugged. "We don't talk about it much."

"Why not?"

"Might scare the tourists," he said.

"I'm not a tourist," I said.

"Haven't seen you around."

"Been away for awhile," I said. "Air Force."

The man looked at me, considering. He was a bit older than me, so he wouldn't have any reason to doubt me really.

He pulled up a stool and sat across from me.

"Sometimes people wander out."

"Out? Out from where?"

He shrugged. "Just out."

I smiled a little. The man sounded like he was weaving a fanciful tale. Maybe for my benefit.

"Out but not in?" I asked, mostly just to be difficult.

"Maybe. But not to my knowledge."

"So people wander out."

"Ladies," he said, sending another shiver down my spine.

"How do you know?"

"They walk right past my door there." He gestured toward the bar door.

I looked over my shoulder. "How do you know they're from the boarding house?"

He shrugged. "Adds up. Only way to explain it."

"Okay," I said. "I'm listening."

"Usually happens during the full moon."

I sat back. Ran a finger along the condensation on my beer bottle. It was a full moon last night, but I had gone into the boarding house and seen the people inside during the blinding light of day.

"Everyone see them?" I asked. Wasn't sure where I was going with this, but just followed my instincts.

"Nah." The bartender stopped to refill another customer's glass. Then settled back onto his stool. "Just a few of us locals."

"Describe them," I said.

"Sure." He leaned forward. "Ladies—young ladies—in long dresses. Those bustle things in the back."

"How many of them have you seen?"

The bartender scratched his head. "They're all similar, but I'd say I've seen four different ones. Maybe three. Maybe five. Hard to say."

"You've had a lot of time to think about this," I said, speaking calmly despite the way my stomach flipped over. He saw four. I had seen four.

The bartender got up to close out someone's tab.

I got the sense that the bartender was making this up for my benefit. Either that or he knew about the young people next door. Maybe he was in on it. I watched him out of the corner of my eye.

I usually had a good sense of people, but I wasn't sure what to make of him. I decided I was wasting my time listening to his fanciful stories.

I pulled out some cash, left it on the bar, and headed out the door while he was occupied.

Going back to the boarding house door, I stood in front of it. Listening.

The clouds shifted away from the moon, letting the moonlight spill over me. It was bright enough that it seemed to overwhelm the street lights.

I thought I heard the steady ticking of a grandfather

clock. I shook my head. There was no way I could hear that over the music coming from the bar next door.

Shaking my head, tired of the speculation, I used all my strength to give the knob a swift turn. I suppose I was thinking I'd just break the lock with sheer force.

But the knob turned so easily and the door opened beneath my shoulder that I practically tumbled inside.

As I took a step forward, the door closed behind me. Dismissing it, I looked around.

I was back in what I now knew to be a boardinghouse. The room was lit only by light from lanterns, but it had a cozy air about it. The empty boarded up room I had stood in earlier was nonexistent.

The grandfather clock standing next to the staircase steadily ticked away the minutes. I nearly jumped when it began to chime the hour. It chimed eight times.

Yet it was nearly two in the morning.

A fire crackled in the fireplace and two ladies sat in front of it, their heads bent over whatever they were doing.

I took another step forward and recognized Andrea. Andrea's attention was focused on the needlepoint in her hands.

I recognized the other girl as one of her sisters, the serious one. She had her attention focused on a book.

There was no one else in the room.

I stood perfectly still. Not sure what to do. I did not want to startle the ladies and yet now that I was here, my curiosity took the lead.

Besides, having talked to Andrea once, I wanted to talk to her again. I was drawn to her.

As I was still contemplating what exactly I should do, Andrea looked up and saw me standing there.

"Mr. Smith," she said, tossing her needlepoint aside and standing up. Even in the soft light, I saw the flush on her face.

"Andrea," I said.

"I didn't hear you come in," she said.

I didn't see how she could possibly not have heard the door slam behind me. But the whole situation was quite strange and inexplicable even.

"Please," she said. "Come and have a seat."

I did as she asked. Went to the sofa and sat across from the two ladies.

The other one, Dakota, was scowling at me.

"Good evening," I said to Dakota with a little smile. It did nothing to soften her expression.

Andrea sat back down and watched me carefully. She held her needlepoint, but her hands were idle.

"I looked for you earlier," she said. This made no sense to me since she was the one who had invited me to leave. Why would she ask me to leave, then declare that she had been looking for me?

"I looked for you, too," I said, then bit my tongue at the look of surprise on her face.Dakota leaned over and whispered something to her sister.

Andrea studied me, seeming to consider her sister's words.

"Is it true?" she asked.

I shook my head. "Is what true?"

"Are you a guest here, too?"

The bartender had said this was a boardinghouse. I didn't understand this whole thing. Didn't have a clue what was going on, but if this was indeed a boardinghouse, then it followed that I would be a guest here. It seemed like a simple way to explain my sudden appearance.

"Yes," I said before I had time to change my mind.

"Then please accept my apologies," Andrea said. "I had assumed..." Her voice trailed off. It seemed she had no logical explanation either.

"No need to apologize," I said.

A shadow of confusion crossed her features, but she soon recovered.

Dakota was still watching me with suspicion.

"We were about to go upstairs," Dakota said, closing her book and setting it aside. "It's late."

Andrea glanced over at her, but didn't say anything.

"Of course," I said. Then it occurred to me that the clock simply had the wrong time. It was an old clock and probably did not even work. Mostly there for decoration. "It is late," I agreed.

Andrea set her needlepoint aside again. "I suppose it is," she said.

She and Dakota stepped away, moving toward the stairs. I did not understand the dynamic between the two of them, but it wasn't for me to know.

Andrea stopped and looked back at me. "Perhaps we can

talk in the morning then," she said. "I can explain the earlier... conversation."

"Absolutely," I said. "I look forward to it."

There was that flush again on her cheeks. It was really quite pretty.

As the two girls went upstairs, I sat on the sofa and wondered what, exactly, I was supposed to do now.

CHAPTER 8
Andrea

MY HEART WAS POUNDING RAPIDLY as Dakota and I slipped into our room. Since we were sharing a room, we had no particular reason to move quietly except that it was late and we were used to trying not to wake others.

The trip across the country had been the most difficult thing we had ever done.

There had been dangers at every turn. Snakes. Illnesses. Accidents.

So many people we had started out with us hadn't made it. It was a wonder the west was being settled at all.

I was grateful that all five of us had made it without any mishaps. I still didn't have a good feel for life out here on the frontier, but if I had to venture a guess, I would say it's about as dangerous out here as it had been on the trail. Maybe not quite as bad... I hope... maybe different kinds of dangers I just hadn't identified yet.

Dakota went straight off to sleep, slipping into her regular light snoring. For such a serious girl, she had no problem shutting off her thoughts and going to sleep.

I, on the other hand, lay awake. I heard the river roaring, coyotes howling, piano music from the saloon down the street.

But all those noises were merely background for my busy thoughts.

Mostly... okay totally... involving a man named Reed Smith.

Earlier, when we had first met, I had told him far more than was appropriate to tell a stranger. I'd thought he was here to represent Dr. Avery, but he was merely a guest just as we were.

I wondered why he hadn't corrected me. He was probably just kind or maybe even confused. Probably a bit of both.

I would talk with him tomorrow at breakfast. Straighten out the misunderstanding.

He was a handsome man. Clean. Educated. Polite.

We had traveled with people who were definitely not clean, including us at that particular time. Unlike us, though, most were not educated. And many were anything other than polite.

It was odd, really, how we ended up out here after traveling along with so many diverse people. But now that we were here, how people just seemed to sort themselves back out.

The wild ones went to the saloon. Some of the poor

ones scattered to the woods to maybe work the earth. Others found shelter somewhere and went to work as laborers.

Then others, educated, polite, and thankfully now clean, like us and Mr. Smith ended up here at the boarding house.

No matter where people went, they seemed to sort themselves back out into their respective places in society.

The full moon cast its bright light through the window. So bright I could see trees limbs blowing in the gentle wind.

I gave up on sleep. With the bright moonlight, the noises from outside, and the loudness of my own thoughts, I tossed in the towel and slid out of bed.

After touching my toes to the cold floor, I put on my socks and boots, then fastened my fur-lined cloak over my shoulders.

I would just go downstairs, have some warm milk, and sit by the fire until I was sleepy.

By the time I reached the top of the stairs, I was wondering where I thought I was going to get warm milk. But I had come too far to turn back now.

I moved quietly, without making a sound, practically gliding down the stairs.

The grandfather clock chimed the hour as I reached the bottom floor.

Maybe Hector was still up and he could heat some milk for me.

If nothing else, I could at least get a glass of water.

Restless. That was the only way to describe how I was feeling.

As a lady, I should be sleeping right now. Not up wandering the house like a floozy.

Especially knowing that there were men about. Not Hector. Hector was staff. But Reed Smith. I knew Reed—a perfect stranger—was here somewhere, yet I persisted in my journey through the house. Alone. In the middle of the night.

I found Hector in the kitchen. Still up, chopping potatoes for tomorrow's breakfast, was more than happy to heat a cup of hot milk for me. I didn't ask where he got the milk. Not only would that be rude, but I had learned that if I was going to eat and survive, I did not need to know where things came from. If I knew such things, I would no doubt eat or drink almost nothing.

Still moving quietly, I left the kitchen, went back into the main room, carefully holding the hot mug in both hands. Hector had taken me at my word when I had asked for *hot* milk. It occurred to me too late that I should have asked for a tray.

Reed was standing in front of the fire, his gaze on the flames. I don't think he knew I was there.

I got as far as the stairs, still trying to decide if I wanted to slip past him to go back upstairs or if I wanted to stick with my original plan to sit by the warm fire.

It seemed a bit bold, with him being there, a perfect stranger and all, to join him.

As I stood there, hesitating, he must have sensed my presence. It certainly wasn't that I made any noise.

Then he turned and looked right at me.

At first, he showed no recognition. No sign that he saw me other than faint surprise.

But now that he had seen me, it would have been rude for me to ignore him and pretend that I had not seen him. Especially since I was obviously looking right at him.

"Good evening," I said. "I hope I'm not disturbing you."

His expression changed. It was as though he suddenly realized I was there.

"Not at all," he said. "Please. Come join me." He stepped aside, leaving room for me to stand next to him.

Again. It would be rude to refuse.

I was nothing, if not well-bred. Manners were the one thing I had an abundance of.

"Thank you," I said. "You're very kind."

But instead of going to stand next to him, I went to the chair closest to the fire and sat down, setting the mug on my knees to give my fingers a break from the scalding heat.

"You couldn't sleep?" he asked.

"Unfortunately, no," I admitted. "My sister snores like a freight train."

He laughed and I caught my breath. His laughter changed his face. I already found him handsome, but with a smile upon his lips, he was none other than dashing.

I was rarely swayed by a dashing man since I was under the impression that dashing men were by nature rakes. It wasn't their fault. It was simply that a handsome man experienced the world differently than a not so handsome man.

Take my brother, for example, he was young now, but I

was certain he was going to be handsome. Already, he was turning young ladies' heads.

And already he was accustomed to getting what he wanted by offering nothing more than a smile.

I had watched this phenomenon and had to confess that I actually used it to our advantage a few times on our trek to get here.

For my brother, the world was a place that gave him what he wanted without too much work. For indeed, how much work was a simple smile.

And that, I decided was how a rake was born.

I planned on finding myself a humble man someday. One who would be content to live a modest life with me. One who would not use his charm for gain.

Having been raised in affluence, I knew that it brought nothing but the illusion of safety. I believed that my parents had been happy, but I was also fairly certain that my father was not a rake.

That a man could be humble and rich at the same time, I didn't doubt.

"What are you thinking about?" Reed asked.

"Nothing," I said, smiling sweetly.

When dealing with a rake, a lady had to keep her thoughts to herself. Not that I had a lot of experience in dealing with rakes.

CHAPTER 9
Reed

I HAD LIED. It had been out of necessity, but I had lied nonetheless.

The fireplace was well stocked with chopped wood and the fire gave off a warm, cozy heat. Dark blue velvet curtains had been pulled closed over the windows leaving the room in darkness other than the glow of the fire.

I stood in the boardinghouse, claiming to be a guest, when in fact, if I wanted to stay here—which I did—I had no place to go.

Since it was more like a bed and breakfast, there was no check-in desk. Going upstairs and attempting to find a room seemed like a poor choice, so I decided that I would sleep on the sofa and sort things out in the morning.

I could have—probably should have—left, of course, and returned to my own cabin.

But now that I was here, I wanted to stay.

I already knew from experience that sometimes I could get in here and sometimes I could not. Although it defied all logic, I didn't think too much about it. There were some things best left alone.

The bottom line was I wasn't ready to leave this place. Wherever this place was. Especially since I didn't know if I could return.

Andrea sat next to me, holding a mug of steaming hot milk.

When I'd first seen her standing next to the stairway, I thought I was seeing a ghost. The bartender's words had flashed back through my mind.

Sometimes they wander out.

Perhaps he meant the ladies I was seeing here in the boardinghouse, Andrea for one.

"I need you to be truthful about something," I said.

She looked up at me from beneath dark, delicate lashes. "I always strive to be truthful," she said with a disarmingly innocent look.

"I'm quite serious," I said.

"What is it you want to know?" she asked, carefully bringing the mug to her lips.

"Are you playing at some kind of game?"

Her brows knit, she looked blankly at me. "Game?"

Perhaps I wasn't going about this quite right.

"Are you supposed to be here?" I waved a hand in a vague direction around the room.

She balanced her cup on her knees. She was wearing a long cloak over what looked like could be a white nightgown and her long brunette hair flowed around her shoulders.

"Does anyone know where they're supposed to be? Looking back on how we ended up here, I wonder if it was meant to be. If we were fated to be here all along." She stared into the flames of the fireplace as she spoke. Her voice soft and contemplative.

Then she looked back up at me, meeting my gaze head on. "But if you are being literal, then yes. We pay our way."

"I'm not sure what I meant," I said, utterly confused about what she was talking about.

"I apologize for earlier. For assuming you were here on Dr. Avery's behalf. It was time for him to be here and you were here... I just assumed."

"It seems like a logical assumption," I said.

"As you can see, our family is quite large and we would like stay here as long as we need to. At least until I can get one of my sisters married off."

I just looked at her. Trying to sort out what exactly she was talking about.

"You want to find a husband for your sister?"

"Yes," she said, then put a hand on her forehead. "There I go. Telling you more than you need or want to know. I don't normally talk to strangers like this. I'm usually quite private."

"Your secrets are safe with me," I said.

"Well then," she said. "It's late and I should try again to sleep." She moved as though to stand up.

"Wait," I said. "Don't go."

She hesitated.

"Stay a little longer. Please."

"Very well," she said. "I can stay until I finish my warm milk."

"Good," I said. "Thank you."

We sat in silence with only the ticking of the grandfather clock to keep us company.

There was something called a shared psychosis. Folie à deux. Perhaps Andrea and her... family... friends—whatever they were—shared some disorder.

Although I had read about it, it wasn't something given much attention, at least not in my training. Mostly because it was quite rare and certainly not likely to be seen on the battlefield.

But here, I decided, was a textbook example of shared psychosis. All I could do, really, was to play along. It wasn't my job to treat her. Knowing a little—very little—about a disorder did not make me qualified. It would be like me attempting heart surgery when I was trained to only measure a person's heart rate.

"How long have you been here?" I asked.

"We arrived three days ago," she said without a hitch. She took another sip of her milk, holding it carefully with her fingertips, then balanced the mug on her knees again.

"Can I hold that mug for you?" I asked.

That brought a small smile to her lips. "I think I've got it."

I sat down in the chair next to hers.

"It looks like it's burning your fingers," I said, holding

out my hands, palms up. The mug had no handles and she was balancing it precariously on her knees with her fingertips.

Surprising me, she handed me her mug. It was a bit warm, but nothing intolerable.

"This is much better," I said, leaning back in my chair.

"How so?" She was adorable when she was perplexed.

"The longer the milk lasts, the longer you will stay."

She looked blankly at me, then smiled.

"You, Sir," she said. "are a rake."

CHAPTER 10
Andrea

I PULLED the warm fur-lined cloak closer around me. I wouldn't tell Reed, but it was nice to have my hands free.

The crackling fire in the huge fireplace was warm and I honestly preferred to stay here instead of going upstairs to my room with no heat. If I were alone, I would curl up on the sofa and tuck my feet beneath the thick cloak. Probably easily fall asleep.

But instead, I was most certainly not alone.

I was sitting here with Reed.

In another world, being here in the middle of the night unchaperoned would be scandalous. Especially since I had just deemed Reed to be a rake.

But we were not in Natchez. And out here there was no one to chaperone. There were no propriety rules to follow. Or so I had been told.

There had been an older woman, her name was Mrs.

Green, who had sort of taken us under her wing, but she had stayed in Denver when we continued on to Whiskey Springs.

She had talked to us about how things would be different out here. I hadn't really believed her at the time. I had no way of knowing, of course, where we were headed.

All I had was a note from my father. I'd found it tucked into one of the books in his private library.

The note had been tucked in the pages of a simple dime novel.

Dear Wife,

If anything happens to me, take the children and go to Whiskey Springs, Colorado Territory. Give the sealed letter herein attached to Dr. Alexander Avery.

Since our mother had succumbed before she could follow our father's wishes... before I even knew about the letter, the task fell to me.

"I've been called a lot of things before," Reed said. "But I've never been called a rake."

The logs shifted in the fireplace, sending sparks up the chimney and scattering them out onto the little rug in front of the hearth.

The grandfather clock steadily keeping track of the seconds, began to chime.

Reed and I sat in silence, looking at each other until after the twelfth chime was no more than an echo in the air.

Midnight. It was already Midnight. And yet I was not ready to leave him.

"I find that hard to believe," I said. "I'm no expert, but I'm pretty sure you have all the makings."

He settled back in his chair, looking like a man who had nowhere else to be and who wanted to be nowhere else.

"What, exactly, are those makings?"

"Well," I said. "For one... You've hijacked my milk."

"I would never intentionally hijack a lady's milk. Not without her permission."

He held out the mug and I took it, wrapping my hands around it.

"Two," I said. "You are far too bold."

"I can't deny that," he said. "Being in the military requires a man to be bold."

"A soldier," I said. "My father fought under General Robert E. Lee."

"I see," he said. "Then you know a lot about being a soldier."

I took a sip of the milk. It was cooler now and not nearly so appetizing. I should just finish it off, but despite my declaration that I would stay until I finished it, I found that I was not ready to go upstairs. I was not ready to leave Reed's company.

I suppose I had a bit of boldness in me as well.

"I only know what I got from his letters. After he left for the army, he only came home one time."

"I'm sorry," he said.

I squared my shoulders. "There was a lot that happened, but we're here now." I looked into his eyes. "We made it and my father would be pleased."

Instead of saying anything else, he held out a hand for

my mug. I handed it to him. There was something oddly intimate about him holding my mug of milk for me.

Good heavens. Was I becoming like my flirty sister, Bailey?

"I should go upstairs now," I said. "It's late."

"Are you sleepy then?"

Was I? Not in the least. Talking with Reed had my blood pumping through my veins and I could not have fallen asleep if I had tried.

"No," I said.

"I should heat your milk again," he said.

"Maybe," I said. I wouldn't mind, but I didn't think it was a good idea to admit this to Reed. A rake would use such information to his advantage. He would think his charm was working on me.

It was, of course, but...

"I'll be right back," he said, setting off toward the kitchen.

Hector may not even be awake by now. But he didn't give me time to stop him.

Still cold, I knelt on the rug in front of the fireplace, wrapping my cloak around me. I held my hands to the flames and waited.

Mesmerized by the flames and the steady ticking of the grandfather clock, my eyelids grew heavy.

Warm from the fire, my belly full of warm milk, I curled up and laid down, resting my cheek against my folded hands. After months of sleeping with one eye open in the back of a wagon, I now felt blissfully safe. On the prairie, I'd never known when a snake would crawl into the wagon or Indians would descend upon us or... there were so many dangers, I could barely keep up with them. And that did not include the unknowns.

I would only rest a moment. Just until Reed came back.

Just for a moment.

Besides, I needed time to think about why I was so drawn to the mysterious man who dressed differently from anyone else I had ever met.

The man with bold eyes that seemed to see right through to my very soul.

CHAPTER 11
Reed

SETTING the mug of hot milk on the end table, I leaned forward and studied the girl curled up sleeping on the floor in front of the fireplace.

So peaceful. Wrapped beneath her cloak, she looked much too serene to disturb.

I pulled the cloak over one of her little booted feet that had come uncovered.

Finding another blanket folded across the couch, I opened it up and laid it over her.

Her bow-shaped lips slightly parted, her hands beneath her cheek, she looked like an angel lying there.

As an officer—former officer—in the Air Force, I was exactly what she accused me of being. A rake. A player in modern terms.

It wasn't that I was trying to be a player, I just avoided

long-term relationships. And I did that by keeping myself company with women who expected nothing more.

So technically, in my mind at least, I was not a player. A player led women on, right?

A man would have to be more careful with a girl like Andrea.

There would be no love 'em and leave 'em kind of deal.

I hadn't been around girls like Andrea since college. And even then, I had hung out with the party girls. The ones who didn't have any expectations.

I'd had a girlfriend, a real one, in high school, but of course that had only lasted a year. It had been, in fact, just before we moved to Alabama where we had been living when my father had been killed.

For me that had been the end of real girlfriends.

It was best for a man to avoid things he didn't want. I kept my eye on the ball. On my military career.

And here I was.

Alone.

I had not expected to get out of the military alive.

I had to admit that I had developed a pretty lonely life-style. Well, as they say, a leopard couldn't change his spots.

Andrea shifted and, opening her eyes, looked right at me.

She smiled just a little and something shifted deep at my core.

Then she closed her eyes and went back to sleep.

Well hell.

What was I supposed to do now?

I couldn't very well leave her alone. She was young and innocent.

I considered picking her up and carrying her up to her room.

But which room was hers? I knew she had family, but she could have a husband. I didn't mind so much for myself, but I didn't want to cause her trouble.

So I just sat there. Standing sentinel over her while she slept.

I was a soldier and even though I hadn't stood guard in quite some time, I could still do it.

There was no way I was going to leave her here unguarded. Whiskey Springs was a decent enough little town, but it was a tourist town.

And even though it was hard to find this place—to get inside this door, I might not be the only man who accidentally wandered in here off the street.

Picking up the warm milk, I took a long drink. I would have preferred something stronger in my drink, but this would do.

The clock chimed once. One o'clock. It was going to be a long night.

CHAPTER 12
Andrea

"DID YOU SLEEP HERE ALL NIGHT?" Dakota asked.

I peeled my eyes open and tried to figure out exactly where *here* was.

I quickly eliminated anywhere involving a wagon including the back of the wagon.

I was, however, not in a bed. Maybe I was on the ground. But it didn't feel like the ground. And I was warm. So that eliminated outside.

Besides, I was not only covered in my cloak, there was blanket over me. I didn't remember how that got there.

Rolling over, I looked up at my sister. She was scowling at me.

"What time is it?" I asked.

"Seven o'clock," she said, putting her hands on her hips. She was fully dressed. And right now she reminded me of our mother.

It was more than a little disconcerting, so I shook it off.

"Why are you up so early?"

"Chickens," she said.

Baffled, I sat up and scowled back at her. "Chickens?"

"Chickens outside our window."

"Well," I said, getting to my feet and straightening my cloak around my shoulders. "At least that means we will have plenty to eat. Including eggs."

"Must you see the good in everything?" she asked.

"And must you see the bad in everything?"

It was a conversation we had automatically. So many times a day it didn't even require conscious thought.

"Are we the only ones up?" I asked. I already knew the answer. Dakota was always the first one up in the mornings. Then me. Then Bailey and Elise. As for Colton, sometimes he slept until noon and sometimes I don't think he went to bed at all.

Dakota just rolled her eyes.

She went to the window and swept back the curtains.

I turned away from the unexpected bright morning light and focused on the fire, still burning strongly.

With Dakota's back to me, I looked around for any sign of Reed. The last I remembered, he had gone off to refill my mug of hot milk.

I must have fallen asleep while he was gone.

I covered my face with my hands. How strange he must think me to have fallen asleep on the floor.

What kind of lady did that?

A lady who had just traveled across the prairie in a

covered wagon. If I could sleep outside in a wagon, then I could sleep on the floor in front of a warm fire. Of course, he wouldn't know that.

I lifted my chin and pushed my hair out of my face. There was nothing I could do about it now.

He had vanished, leaving me here. Who could blame him, really?

I should be grateful. It was the best night's sleep I had had in as long as I could remember. Even better than the soft, but cold bed upstairs.

I had felt warm and safe here, I suppose.

Yes. I should be grateful for Reed leaving me here. He probably hadn't even seen me here on the floor. He would have thought I had gone back up to my room like a normal person.

I glanced toward the stairs. Perhaps he was even up now.

"I'm going upstairs to get dressed," I said.

"I'll check on breakfast," Dakota said.

For someone who saw only the negative in having her sleep disturbed by chickens, she was awfully quick to be worried about having proper food to eat.

I dashed upstairs, hoping to get to my room and dressed before running into Reed again.

CHAPTER 13
Reed

I walked along the riverbank on my way back to my cabin. The water splashed and burbled as it rushed over the rocks.

The mid-morning sun was warm on my head. It wouldn't be much longer before the first snowfall and then it would be cold.

It occurred to me that I had never seen Whiskey Springs in any season other than summer.

It also occurred to me that the clock in the boarding-house most definitely did not work. It had only been just after six o'clock when I had slipped out the front door, but now it was nearing noon.

When I had seen one of Andrea's sisters coming down the stairs, I had slipped out the front door. The town was already bustling with tourists. Already crowded.

When I'd stepped out onto the sidewalk, no one had even noticed me. I'd stepped from a perfectly quiet building out into a town bustling with traffic. Both vehicles and people on foot.

It had been a strange night.

Since I had taken it on as my job to guard Andrea, I hadn't slept. I could not remember the last time I had spent that many hours awake with absolutely nothing to occupy myself other than my own thoughts.

I had my phone with me, but the battery was dead. I know I'd had it charged, but the battery had been drained.

So with no television. No phone. I'd had nothing to do but sit and think.

I reminded myself that I had come here to do just that, but with the advent of cell phones, a part of me believed that all independent thinking came to a halt.

We, at least most Americans, had our thoughts linked together by the Internet. That was my theory anyway. A few people managed to break through and have independent thoughts, but those thoughts only went into the Internet hopper and became part of the collective thought process.

At any rate, I'd found it almost impossible to *think* without the Internet on my phone to guide that thinking.

So it had been an interesting night.

An elk dashed across the path in front of me, sending low-hanging branches flying. I stopped and waited for the next one.

A couple of moments later, right on cue, two more followed.

I'd lived all over the country and had even been overseas,

but I'd never been anywhere more beautiful and peaceful than right here in this area of the country.

And yet, even after having all night to think, I was no closer to knowing which way to turn next. If anything, I was more discombobulated than I had been before.

I'd replayed the day. My conversations with people. My experiences.

I tried to figure out how I had gotten where I was. In a boardinghouse with a woman who seemed to think she was in the 1800s.

It would not have been so bad, except that I was intrigued by her.

I wanted to know more about her. Everything about her.

It wasn't just curiosity about her having a rare psychological disorder. It was more than that. It was her perfectly serene green eyes.

The way she gazed at me. As though she also wanted to know about me.

I felt it. That pull of attraction.

I didn't want to.

She was too complicated.

Now that I was *retired*... If I was going let myself fall for somebody and maybe start a normal relationship with someone and maybe a family, then it stood to reason that I would need to start out by finding a *normal* woman.

Couldn't start a normal relationship without the basics. Not that I was normal. I had problems of my own.

I rarely slept through the night without waking from a nightmare. In a cold sweat. My sheets all tumbled.

Reaching my cabin, I pulled out my key and let myself in.

Even after I switched on the lights, the cabin felt cold and lonely.

I went to the kitchen and turned on the coffeemaker. If I'd been thinking, I would have stopped in town for a coffee, but it hadn't occurred to me. I was used to getting coffee on base.

Everything in my life was different now.

I was going to have to adjust. To adapt.

And I knew even as I told myself I needed to settle down and start figuring out where I wanted to live. What kind of work I wanted to do to keep myself occupied.

I knew that I was going to be going back to the boardinghouse.

I knew that I wasn't going to be able to stay away from Andrea.

CHAPTER 14
Andrea

A NOTE HAD COME today from Dr. Alexander Avery. He apologized for missing our appointment yesterday. A trapper who lived up the mountain had been injured and he had to go to his assistance.

Sitting at the vanity in the bedroom I shared with Dakota, I refolded the note and tucked it in my valise with my other letters.

My siblings didn't know the details of what I was doing. Heck, I didn't know the details of what I was doing.

I was merely following directions. Father was taking care of us even now that he was gone.

All I really knew was that I was waiting for Dr. Avery. To give him a letter and hopefully make a deal with him that would allow us to survive until we either found jobs or husbands.

That brought me back to the thought I had yesterday.

Bailey needed a husband. Since she was only one year younger than me, she was certainly of age, so that wouldn't be a problem.

All four of my siblings had again gone for a walk this morning. I had stayed behind to wait for Dr. Avery. They had been gone less than thirty minutes when the note had arrived.

I sighed. I would have gladly joined my siblings on their walk around town, but I didn't know which direction they might have taken.

Left to my own devices, I wandered over to the stack of blank canvases that belonged to Bailey.

I took one of her charcoals and her sketchbook, settled into a big chair next to one of the windows in the library and found a blank page.

Looking out at the majestic Rocky Mountains, I began some light sketching. I captured the tree line on the snow-capped mountain range. The jagged, dangerous peaks.

Whiskey Springs was in a valley, but it was high enough in elevation that the mountains looked like they just right over there. Almost within arm's reach.

I would never forget how we had traveled toward these very same mountains for a full week. It seemed like we would never reach them until suddenly we were there.

I sketched in a cabin nestled at the base of the mountains. The sun shifted and I was left to my own imagination.

I added in a little burbling river in front of the cabin, this time drawing on my memory from the road—no more than a trail really—leading to Whiskey Springs.

I let my thoughts wander as I sketched.

I had not seen Reed all day.

Hector had looked at me with a strange expression when I'd asked him if he had seen Reed today. Since he didn't seem to know who Reed was, I hadn't said anything further.

After the way he had vanished out the front door that first time I had seen him, I was already hesitant to ask much about him.

Besides, it would be unseemly for me to show eagerness at seeing a rake such as Reed. He no doubt had any number of female admirers vying to become his wife.

I certainly did not want to be in the category with them. I was not in the market for a husband and even if I were, I would not entertain the idea of marrying a rake.

I preferred my loosely held plan of marrying a modest man one day. A man whose words I could trust. A man who would be at my side both day and night.

The main door to the boardinghouse opened and the animated voices of my sisters drifted through the halls of the house.

I used a soft cotton cloth to wipe the charcoal off my hands and looked down at my drawing.

My sister, Dakota, was the one with the artistic passion. Or more to the point, she was the one whose talent was recognized.

I had the talent, but not the passion. I had, in fact, yet to find my passion.

But as I looked at my drawing with an objective eye, I decided it wasn't half bad. It was actually pretty good.

There was, however, one problem. I had not merely sketched a bucolic mountain scene with a log cabin, I had unconsciously sketched a portrait.

A reasonably accurate likeness of Reed.

And even his image on paper, one that I had drawn myself, set my blood racing through my veins.

A rake, indeed.

CHAPTER 15
Reed

AFTER A QUICK NAP, I showered, put on a clean pair of jeans and a white button-down shirt, then walked back to town.

I wore military issued combat boots, my most comfortable footwear for walking and carried my now fully charged iPhone.

There was a coolness to the air and clouds hovered around the mountaintops. The scent of fir and spruce trees was strong. Refreshing. Like walking in a candle shop in the mall.

I grabbed a late lunch-early dinner and wandered the streets. Not as many tourists out. It was nearing the end of the season and it seemed like there were fewer of them every day. It was significantly quieter, too. One of those days when the tourists were subdued.

I didn't look for the door that led to the mysterious

boardinghouse.

Instead, I just spent some time becoming accustomed to being a regular civilian. In effect, I blended.

But even though I blended, I didn't *feel* ordinary. It wasn't just my status as a newly retired veteran. It was my experience with Andrea that had me feeling off-balance.

I caught interested glances from more than one woman. One was a clerk in a souvenir store packed with t-shirts and coffee mugs and overpriced sunshades. Another was a cute little blonde server in the café where I ate alone. And one was a curvy tourist with a young son, not more than five.

Under normal circumstance, I might have pursued the clerk and maybe the server. If not for the child, the tourist could have been fun to do some exploring around town with. Maybe more. Maybe more, with or without the child. On two different paths except for one thing.

Andrea.

She was front and center in my brain, effectively blocking any energy I might have had for more than a passing glance at anyone else.

As I walked through the little park tucked behind some of the shops, red and gold aspen trees quaking in the soft breeze, I considered what had happened.

Andrea and I had shared no more than a brief conversation. And then there were the few hours I had spent watching her sleep.

Nothing life-altering. At least nothing that should have been life-altering.

And yet... I could not stop thinking about her.

To say that Andrea was an old-fashioned girl would clearly be an understatement.

I hadn't so much as looked at an innocent girl since high school.

And I had also avoided any serious entanglements.

As a military man, I had promised myself that I would not have a family unless I could offer stability. And to me stability meant having a house. Maybe in the suburbs. Where the kids could start off in first grade and go all the way through high school graduation with the same friends.

Like normal people. I had never had that. I had met a lot of people and had a lot of adventures, but I always felt like I had missed out on having stability.

So I had tucked thoughts of a family away, deep in the recesses of my mind. A family was something for other people.

I watched a young couple, hand in hand walking through the park, their heads bent together, talking and laughing. And I wondered just how much I had missed by not allowing myself to have an actual girlfriend.

I stopped on a little wooden bridge over the burbling river and watched a fish swimming about, searching for something to eat.

A mother duck and two ducklings following close behind her waddled to the edge of a little pond with a fountain and jumped right in. The mother duck showed them how to put their heads down in the water. They came up, heads shaking, giving me a laugh.

I don't know why, but watching the ducks frolicking in the water relieved some of the tension I had been feeling.

Walking along the river path, I picked up a pebble and tossed it into the water.

It occurred to me, in that moment, watching the ripples in the water, that it was possible, not likely, but possible that the door I had found to the boardinghouse was a portal to the past.

As I squinted against a haze created by the sun glinting off the water, a memory flashed back.

My grandmother on my mother's side, Sophia Becquerel, used to tell my sisters and me stories at bedtime. We loved it that she told stories, making them up as she went, instead of reading them.

One of her stories was about how her grandmother's life had been saved by an old Indian.

The girl, Vaughn Becquerel, had been traveling from France to marry a man... a stranger... when her traveling party had been attacked by hostile Indians.

Vaughn had been the only one in her traveling party to survive. There was one of the Indians, an old one, who had saved her life by casting a spell.

Because of that spell, she had survived by going into the future through a rip in time. From the 1700s to the 1800s.

The spell had saved her life by sending her through time.

Though I hadn't thought about this for years, my grandmother's words came back to me just as clearly as though she was standing next to me.

Vaughn's life was saved by the spell that made a rip in

time. But there was a catch. The rip in time never healed. It was passed on to those of her blood. They, too, would travel through time.

I shook my head.

Those of her blood.

A fancy way of saying her descendants.

And I was one of those descendants.

CHAPTER 16
Andrea

FEELING cross about not only had my errant siblings finally made their way home in time for supper, but also that my unconscious had betrayed me by putting an image of Reed on paper, I sat with at the dining room table with my family.

I sat at the head of the table, not for any particular reason other than Dakota had sat on one side of me and Elise on the other. It was also how the table had been set. Two seats left at the other end of the table.

Bailey sat wearing the new bonnet she had bought yesterday and now Elise had one, too. So they had gone shopping while they were out. I was afraid to ask what Bailey had bought today, although I was certain it was something and that she would tell before the food was served.

Hector brought out a tray of baked chicken and beans. Set it in the center of the table. Beans, as well as biscuits, appeared to be a staple of food out here in the west. At least it was beans tonight and not peas.

"Did Dr. Avery come by?" Dakota asked. At least one of my siblings thought to ask.

"No," I said. "He sent a note, stating that he had to make a house call."

"What did you do all day?" Dakota asked.

I daydreamed about a mysterious rake who has hijacked my thoughts. "I did some sketching."

"I wondered where my sketchpad was," Bailey said.

I had stashed it in one of my trunks until I had time to tear my drawing from her pad.

"I hope you don't mind," I said.

"Of course not," Bailey said, but I could tell that she wasn't ecstatic about it. She had to know that I would buy her another sketchpad when that one ran out.

"I'm glad you're doing something," Elise said.

"What does that mean?" I asked.

"You just don't seem to ever do anything." Elise said it in such an off-hand way. I could tell she meant no offense, but truly, did my siblings truly think that I never did anything?

Any retort I had been preparing to make dissipated when Reed came to the dining room door.

He stood there a moment, taking everything in, then when his eyes lit on me, he grinned.

Feeling the heat rise to my cheeks, I lowered my head, distractedly stirring my beans.

"Do you have room for one more?" he asked.

"Of course," Colton said, tapping the back of the chair next to him.

I looked up, expecting my sisters to be looking for answers to my reaction, but instead, they had barely even noticed that Reed had come into the room. They certainly had not seen our exchange.

In fact, as Reed took a seat next to Colton, Dakota and Elise were arguing about one of the women they had met in town.

"She definitely liked Colton," Dakota said.

"She was just being nice," Elise said, in her usual innocent, bubbly way.

Dakota rolled her eyes. "Nice my—"

"Dakota," I interrupted her before she could embarrass all of us.

"You weren't there," Dakota said. "She was flirting with her fan."

"Her fan?" I echoed distractedly, watching Reed out of the corner of my eyes. Did anyone even do that anymore?

Reed was three seats down on my left. There was Dakota, then Colton, then Reed. He was right in the thick of my family.

And right now his attention was on Bailey who was sitting directly across from him.

Batting her long, naturally luscious eyelashes at him as was Bailey's nature.

Hector walked around with a pitcher of water, filling our glasses as needed.

He stopped to pick up Elise's napkin that had fallen to the ground.

I watched all this with a valiant attempt at keeping myself from staring at Reed.

He was a guest here, just as we were, and like us, he had every right to eat his supper in peace.

I sipped my water, my barely touched plate of food forgotten on the table in front of me.

"Andrea?"

Elise put a hand on my wrist, jarring my attention back to the present.

"What is it?" I asked, turning to my youngest sister.

"Hector," she said with a quick nod to my left.

"You have a visitor, Miss," Hector said.

"A visitor?" Who would be calling on me in the evening? Who would be calling on me in Whiskey Springs at all for that matter.

"It's Dr. Avery," Hector said.

"Of course." I set my glass down. "I've been expecting him. Please excuse me," I said to no one in particular as I stood up.

Reed was watching me intently.

My heart was pounding dangerously, but I didn't know if I was because I was finally about to meet Dr. Avery to discuss my family's future or if it had anything to with the way Reed was watching me.

If I were a betting woman, which I was not, I would have put my money on the latter.

CHAPTER 17
Reed

I HADN'T TOUCHED the beans, chicken, or biscuits on my plate. I had eaten already, but it would have been rude to refuse. To my credit, I had every intention of eating everything on my plate, but I felt like I was watching history unfold in front of my very eyes.

A quick search on my phone's Internet had led to a trip to the Whiskey Springs Library.

Proud of their heritage, they had everything I was looking for and more.

After three hours spent with my head deep in old books, I had answers. I had answers to questions I didn't even know I had.

And I had irrefutable support for my theory.

The Auclair family had settled in Whiskey Springs in 1866, just after the Civil War.

When I first found that little piece of information, I was

impressed by the attention to detail these reenactors had gone to.

But then I had seen the pictures. Replicating dress, mannerisms, and personality was one thing, but actually looking like someone else was quite another.

All five of the Auclair siblings sitting here at the table with me *looked* like the ones in the pictures. That could not be chance.

Once that had time to sink in, I read everything I could find and then and only then did I make my way to the door to the boardinghouse.

It had opened easily, almost like it had been waiting to invite me in.

I was being fanciful, of course. Something I, as a soldier, had not been allowed. But remembering the stories told me by my grandmother and then looking through the books I found in the library, reading every tidbit of information I could find, I gave myself permission.

Excusing myself and following Andrea into the parlor to meet Dr. Avery solidified everything for me.

The famous Dr. Alexander Avery, one of the founders of Whiskey Springs, stood in front of the fireplace, his hands behind his back.

Andrea looked over her shoulder. Saw me. But didn't say anything.

Dr. Avery came forward.

"It's a pleasure to meet you, Miss Auclair," he said, taking her hand briefly, before looking at me questioningly.

"This is my... friend, Mr. Smith," Andrea said.

"Pleasure to meet you," I said, stepping forward to shake Dr. Avery's hand.

The three of us sat in the chairs in front of the fireplace and just like that I had integrated myself into what I was coming to accept had to be the past.

"I have a letter for you," Andrea told Dr. Avery. "From my father."

"I was genuinely saddened to hear of his passing," Dr. Avery said.

"You knew?"

"Yes. Your father and I served together. He was a good man."

"Thank you," she said, lowering her gaze.

Hector came into the room. "Here's the letter you asked me to get, Miss," he said.

"Thank you, Hector. You're very kind."

Andrea took the letter from Hector and handed it to Dr. Avery.

"You don't have to read it now," she said.

"Do you know what's it's about?" he asked with a glance at me.

I shook my head.

"No," Andrea said. "I suppose I could have opened it, but I didn't want to open something that could be personal between you and my father."

"It must be important for him to send his daughter across the country to deliver a letter."

She glanced at me, looking a bit uncomfortable.

"It was actually attached to another letter. One

instructing us to come here if something were to happen."
She paused. "If we had nowhere else to go."

"I take it that happened," he said, his expression
softening.

She nodded.

"In that case," he said. "I'm very sorry to hear it."

CHAPTER 18
Andrea

AFTER DR. AVERY LEFT, taking the letter with him, I felt a strange sense of what I could only describe as loss.

I had carried that letter all the way from Mississippi to Whiskey Springs. I regretted, now, not opening it.

But now it was too late. And I had no idea what my father had written to Dr. Avery. Or why.

I sat very still after he left. Reed moved over to sit next to me.

"Are you okay?" he asked.

I looked into his bluest of blue eyes. I'd been better. But with him here, I had been worse. He took the edge off. Distracted me.

"I should have opened the letter," I said.

He nodded. "Most people would have," he said. "But you not opening it makes you special."

I blew out a breath. "Special, all right."

Laughing, he put a hand over mine.

That simple touch sent all sorts of shivers through me. Shivers that made butterflies in my stomach go crazy.

"I admire you for it," he said. "I don't think I could have done it."

"Now I feel really stupid."

"Don't," he said. "Dr. Avery seems like a good man. I think he'll read the letter and let you know what it says. In fact..." He looked at me with consideration. "I think he'd let you read it if you asked him. Maybe even give it back for you to keep."

"That helps," I said. "I will. I'll ask him. It would mean a lot for me to know what my father wanted to say to him. I feel like it must have been important."

"I agree," he said.

"How long are you planning to stay here?" I asked. "In Whiskey Springs?"

"I don't know yet. How long do you think I should stay?"

I'd almost forgotten that he was a rake. But his words reminded me.

"I think that is entirely up to you," I said.

"You could have something to do with it," he said.

Bold. Charming. Charming and bold.

My sister Bailey would be a good match for him.

Even as the thought occurred to me, I quickly dismissed it. I didn't like the way it made me feel. I didn't want him to court Bailey.

I wanted him for myself.

What did it say about me that I was attracted to a rake?

Just as the clock chimed the hour, Dakota peaked into the room.

"Can we come in now?" she asked.

"Of course," I said. It was just like Dakota to be the fearless one who would lead the charge for my other three siblings.

Sometimes I think she would have been a good older sister. But then she and I shared a lot of qualities, so one of us may have been about like the other. We were both responsible and serious. She just happened to be suspicious of everything and everyone.

Bailey, Colton, and Elise followed her into the room.

"I should go," Reed said, letting go of my hand.

"Don't go," Colton said. "You can pair up with Andrea to give us three teams."

I glared at my younger brother, but he appeared to be clueless.

Reed didn't want to stay here with us and play games.

"What are we playing?" Reed asked.

I tried to keep my groan of embarrassment to myself. Reed was a grown man. Not a man who would want to play games.

"Let's play the flying game," Elise said. Of course. It was her favorite.

There were several groans. I wasn't the only one who didn't really care for the flying game, but everyone acquiesced. Elise, being the baby, was spoiled. By all of us. Even self-centered Bailey. Maybe especially Bailey, oddly enough.

"How do we play?" Reed asked, standing up.

Elise stepped up. And before I knew it, she had Reed and Colton dragging five wooden chairs from the kitchen and lining them up in a semicircle.

I wanted to crawl under the table itself as she explained the game to Reed.

"Every time I say the name of an animal that can fly, you flap your arms. Like this." She lifted her arms out to her sides and flapped them like wings.

"Ready?" She put her arms down. "Bird." She kept her arms down while we lifted ours.

All five of us flapping our arms, then lowering them.

"Owl."

We lifted our arms again.

"Butterfly."

Arms back up.

"Cat."

We all kept our arms down this time.

Sitting on the end, next to Reed, I had a clear view of everyone.

"Penguin."

My excuse was that I wasn't really paying attention. And Colton, devil that he was, faked me out. He lifted his shoulders like he was going to lift his arms, but of course, he didn't.

And I was the only one flapping my arms. Go figure.

Elise laughed out loud. "Penguins can't fly," she said.

"It was an accident," I said only loud enough for Reed to hear.

He just grinned.

"What's the forfeit?" Bailey asked.

"Let's do the three questions," Dakota said.

I looked at Reed. "I'll be back," I said with resignation. I messed up. I had to pay the penalty.

CHAPTER 19
Reed

I WAS ENJOYING MYSELF IMMENSELY.

I could not remember the last time I had played an innocent game. Maybe even not since I was a child.

Five minutes after Andrea dutifully hid in the kitchen, her siblings had three questions ready for her to answer.

Apparently, the game was that she had to answer yes or no before she even knew what the questions were. To their credit, they wrote them down to avoid any kind of cheating.

I learned a lot about the four of them while they put together their questions.

"What are your answers?" Elise asked the minute Andrea walked back into the parlor.

"No. No. And no," she said without hesitation, sitting down in her chair and waiting for the questions.

And her siblings knew her well. They had predicted that she would answer no to all of them.

"Told you," Dakota said.

"Yes," Bailey said. "She knows we know that, so sometimes she answers yes."

"True," Dakota said. "But she's distracted, so I told you she would say no."

Bailey looked at her with new interest, but didn't say anything.

Colton went first. "Will you eat a bug?"

Andrea wrinkled her nose. "You don't have a bug. What if I had said yes?"

Colton grinned. "I knew you would say no. And, trust me, I could find a bug for you to eat."

"My turn," Elise said. "Will you bark like a dog?"

The color drained out of Andrea's face. I could only imagine how embarrassed that would have made her if she had said yes.

"One more," Dakota said, handing the list of questions to Bailey.

"Will you NOT show us the drawing you made today in my sketchbook?"

"She said *no!*" Elise happily twirled around in a little circle.

"We get to see your drawing," Bailey said with a wide grin.

Andrea was shaking her head. "It's not worth showing," she said. Her face was unusually pale.

"Why don't we skip this one?" I asked, feeling a need to come to her rescue.

"We can't skip it," Elise said. "It's against the rules.

Andrea was pale, but she kept her chin high. "Fine," she said, looking at me sideways.

"Ask me one," I said, standing up. "I'll answer a question in her stead."

The four siblings looked at each other.

"Is that a thing?" Colton asked.

They all looked at Elise, since it was her game, after all.

"Why not?" she said. "Yes or no?" She looked at me with a challenge in her eyes.

"Don't you have to write the question down first?" I asked.

"Very well," Elise said, snatching the paper from Bailey. Her skirts rustling, she went to the little writing desk and scribbled something. She used the feather pen like a pro.

I stood next to Andrea. Waiting for Elise to determine our fate. Andrea looked straight ahead, her brow furrowed in consternation.

"Should I say yes or no?" I bent close and whispered.

She looked up at me, her eyes wide, as though I had startled her. "I usually say no," she said, licking her lips. "But obviously it sometimes backfires on me."

Elise came back, holding the paper with satisfaction. "Yes or no?" That challenge was still there.

I had the fleeting thought that these were strong women. The backbone of the frontier.

"Yes," I said, deciding on the spot that whatever it was, it couldn't be that bad and I would just do it, appeasing the blood-thirsty siblings.

Bailey crossed her arms with a smug look of satisfaction. "Will you kiss Andrea?"

CHAPTER 20
Andrea

I<small>T</small> <small>WAS</small> quiet enough in the house to hear a pin drop. Even the ticking of the grandfather clock seemed to fade.

Or maybe that was just me.

I was thankful I was sitting down as my pesky sister Bailey read her question out loud.

Will you kiss Andrea?

And even though he had said yes, he had said yes before he even knew the question.

The rules of the game included not embarrassing anyone. At least not too bad.

Whatever had possessed her to ask Reed to kiss me?

When Reed had bent close to whisper in my ear, he was close enough to smell. He smelled like the leather of old books, mixed with maybe vanilla, and something earthy I couldn't put a name to.

Whatever it was, it had my stomach full of drunk butterflies again.

The warmth of the fire was too much. My face felt flushed and I felt a little bit dizzy.

I couldn't bring myself to look at Reed.

All four of my siblings were watching us. While Bailey looked smug, the others looked confused. Even Colton looked perplexed.

"You said yes," Bailey said.

"Yes," Reed said. "I did. And you may not realize it, but I am a man of my word."

I clasped my hands tightly in my lap.

I was going to kill them. Every single one of them. Bailey especially.

I glared at my sister, but she was not the least bit intimidated. She just smiled impishly.

Reed leaned close.

Then he kissed me on the cheek.

I was doomed.

Falling in love with a rake.

As he straightened, my siblings clapped.

"Let's play something else," Dakota said.

I opened my eyes and gave Dakota a grateful look.

"I need some air," I said.

When I stepped out the back door, I immediately had regrets. The air was cold. Like the coldest of a Mississippi winter day.

I had a feeling that for here in Whiskey Springs, this was hardly cold at all.

Shivering, I rubbed my arms, but my thin cotton dress was no defense against the chilly air.

Nonetheless, I was determined to stay out here for at least a few minutes.

I walked to the edge of the porch and looked up at the full moon.

It was funny. It looked exactly like it did in Mississippi. How was that possible?

"It's beautiful, isn't it?" Reed asked, coming up behind me.

I looked over my shoulder.

"I brought you something," he said, holding up my fur-lined cloak.

"Thank you," I said, slipping into my cloak while he held it for me.

"How does this work?" he asked, holding both ends of the clasp at my neck.

"It's easy," I said, looking down at his hands.

"Show me," he said.

Our fingers brushed as I took the two sides of the clasp from him and hooked it together.

"I should apologize for my sisters and my brother," I said. When the wind tousled my hair into my eyes, I turned away from it.

"Please don't," he said. "I was really enjoying them."

Warm in my cloak, but my breath misty in the air and my nose no doubt red from being cold, I looked at him.

"Surely you jest," I said.

He smiled. "No. Coming out of the... military, I'd forgotten what it was like to be around a normal family."

"Your family?" I asked.

He looked up at the moon, a sadness settling on his features. "No," he said. "My father didn't survive the war. And my mother still lives in Alabama. My sister... I don't even really know where she is."

"I'm sorry," I said. "It was hard when we lost our parents. But we have each other."

"Yes," he said. "You do have each other. That's a very special gift."

"I know," I said, with a shiver.

"We should go back inside," he said. "Get you some warm milk from the kitchen."

I smiled and bit my lip.

He tucked a strand of hair out of my eyes, then held out his hand.

CHAPTER 21
Reed

I CONSIDERED MYSELF A QUICK STUDY, but learning to heat milk on an iron stove while trying to look like I knew what I was doing was a bit challenging.

Andrea sat at the table, still wrapped in her cloak.

Her siblings were in the parlor. Apparently they had no problem continuing their entertainment without her. Such was the way of being the oldest child, I suppose.

But she didn't seem concerned about it.

"You have a lot of responsibility," I said as we watched the milk begin to boil and listened to her sisters giggling.

"I guess I do," she said. "I don't really think about it."

"We just do what we have to do, right?" I was thinking about my own service in the military. And the way they had just up and decided it was time for me to retire.

"I guess so."

"I admire you," I said and I meant it, but I wanted to see

her happy. To take the responsibility off her shoulders and allow her to enjoy life. To be carefree like her sisters.

As the milk began to boil, the clock chimed the hour. Seven o'clock.

But I wasn't in a position to do that.

Even if I was, well... I wasn't.

I should tell her.

I poured the milk from the boiler into the mug and handed it to her. Then I poured one for myself.

But telling her that I was from the future might be more than she could handle right now. She had a lot going on with watching after her younger siblings.

And somehow, though I was unclear on how it happened, she was going to be a very successful and important woman here in Whiskey Springs.

The wind howled around the corners of the house, sounding quite eerie.

That eeriness jolted me and I froze, a hand wrapped around the mug of hot milk.

When I had followed Andrea outside, I had remained in this time. I hadn't thought about it in the moment, but it had been completely dark with only moonlight to break the darkness.

No streetlights. No traffic sounds. None.

Even at my cabin on the river, I could hear a layer of background noise. Vehicles on the highway, mostly, and at all hours of the night.

If I was going to stay here, I needed a livelihood. My retirement money would not be available to me. So that left me with the clothes on my back. The cell phone, worthless, in my pocket.

And here I was entertaining thoughts of taking care of Andrea.

I knew how to triage and administer first aid. How to get in difficult situations and bring people out of them to safety.

Maybe that was the answer.

I needed to talk to Dr. Avery.

Perhaps he needed an assistant.

My mind raced.

I might be here to stay.

And if I was, I could survive.

I had so many unanswered questions.

Andrea smiled at me over her mug.

But there was one question I could answer. A question I didn't even know I had until this moment.

I wanted to stay.

CHAPTER 22
Andrea

THE NEXT MORNING, I was up first, as always.

It was quiet outside. Sounded like the wind had died down after last night's wind storm.

Fortunately, Hector already had the fire going, pushing the cold away, at least downstairs. Upstairs was a different story. I wasn't sure how we were going to sleep up there. At home, we had fireplaces in every room.

But those were different days. Forward. We had to keep moving forward.

Hector had said something about bed warmers. I was not unfamiliar with those. So I'd have to become reacquainted with such things.

I went into the kitchen, also warm from the stove to find Hector there, pulling a pan of biscuits out of the oven.

"Good morning," I said. "When do you sleep?"

"Ah," Hector said, smiling over his shoulder. "An old man like me doesn't need much sleep."

I doubted that was true, but I let it go. I was wondering how we could keep him on if we bought the house. It didn't make sense for me to take on work only to pay someone else.

Perhaps all five of us would have to chip in and keep the house going. Doing the work. But none of us were particularly inclined toward cooking, so maybe it would be worth it to keep Hector here.

"It was stormy last night," I said, sitting at the table and taking a bite of biscuit.

"It's blowing in winter," he said.

It took me a minute to understand what he meant by that. "Really? Is that how it works?"

"That's how it works. It'll be snowing before you know it. Then only the trappers will be able to leave town."

"Why is that?"

"The road will be blocked with snow," he said. "And they know how to survive in such conditions."

I knew that we would be trapped here once winter came. People had talked about it as we crossed the prairie. But being here. Experiencing it was another thing altogether.

It wasn't like we had anywhere to go, I reminded myself.

And that thought was immediately chased by the thought that Reed would be stuck here, too. All winter.

That put a smile on my face and I replayed the kiss he had gently pressed on my cheek last night. I had already replayed it about a thousand times. Fallen asleep thinking about it. Woke up thinking about it.

Somewhere along the way, I had given up on trying to resist falling for a rake. Rakes could be reformed. I'd read somewhere that rakes made the best husbands.

That was something I didn't understand. But then there were a lot of things I didn't understand. My mother had passed before she had a chance to tell me all the secrets of marriage.

I was surprised when Bailey, fully dressed—her bright yellow and green dress with a big bow in the back—came into the kitchen.

"What are you doing up so early?" I asked.

She slid into one of the chairs across from me while Hector put together a plate for her.

"Maybe I wanted to talk to you."

"Okay," I said, with obvious wariness.

Bailey was closest to Elise. She and I were cordial, but I couldn't remember the last time we had a serious conversation. Maybe not ever.

"What do you want to talk to me about?"

"Reed."

I set down my fork and straightened, steeling myself. "What about him?" There was no way my sister could know how much I was thinking about him.

As far as she knew, I was completely unconcerned about Reed. Just another guest at the boardinghouse.

"Are you going to marry him?"

"What?" I asked, sincerely shocked. "Why would you ask me something like that?"

She shrugged and took a bite of eggs. "He seems to like you and I know you like him."

I narrowed my eyes at her. "You know no such thing."

"I know plenty," she said.

"You're a mind reader now?" I asked, trying to brush her off.

"I don't have to be," she said.

Then she leaned forward, her fork in midair, lowering her voice. "I saw your drawing."

"What drawing?" Of course, I knew perfectly well what drawing she was talking about.

There was that smug look on her face again.

I sat back. "You saw that drawing before the parlor game."

"Of course I did."

"You should have your hide tanned."

"I think that's outside your purview," she said, seeming to give it some thought. "Anyway, I think you should do it."

I gaped at her before I remembered to close my mouth.

CHAPTER 23
Reed

I WENT into the boardinghouse through the back door. I chose the back door simply because the front door made me wary. Sometimes it was there. Sometimes it wasn't.

But things had certainly been different. If I had any doubt about which century I was in before, I had no doubt now.

There were no cars. No buses. No electricity.

Everything was horses and carriages and women wearing long dresses.

Dirt roads. Wooden sidewalks.

I'd gone out the back door, too. It seemed to be what people who were guests here at the boardinghouse for any length of time did.

Not that I was a guest, I reminded myself.

Since I didn't have a room, I had slept on the sofa. Going to sleep late and waking up before sunrise so no one noticed.

But I had to admit, things were looking up.

When I walked into the parlor, I was met with a peaceful scene. It was only then that I realized I had been holding my breath. Hoping that after leaving here, I could return.

Now that I had decided I wanted to stay in this time, I didn't want to risk it. I didn't want to return to the future.

There was a warm fire in the fireplace. The grandfather clock steadily marking the minutes.

My eyes lit first on Andrea. She was curled up on the sofa, an open book in her hands. Her lips were parted slightly as she focused on the words.

A kindred spirit, she was, getting lost in a book that way.

Then I noted that her sister Dakota sat in a chair, also in front of the fireplace, but her hands were busy with some kind of needlework.

They were the only ones in the room. I didn't want to disturb them, but since I had no room upstairs, I had to either go back in the kitchen or join them in the parlor.

The decision was quickly made for me.

"Good morning," Dakota said, looking up.

"Good morning," I said, putting a pleasant smile on my lips.

Andrea nearly dropped her book. I didn't know if that was a good sign or a bad one. Either she was happy to see me or she wasn't. I honestly could not tell. Either way she was definitely startled.

Our conversation last night had been interrupted by her siblings who had joined us in the kitchen for an evening desert of fresh apple pie.

After that, much like the night before, her sister Dakota had suggested that it was bedtime.

But unlike last night, Andrea had agreed and had gone with them.

"I didn't mean to startle you," I said, going to the fireplace and removing the gloves and coat I had borrowed from Hector. They weren't his. But whose ever they were, he seemed to have the stewardship over them. Since this was a boardinghouse, it was logical that there would be things like extra clothes on hand.

"It's cold outside," Andrea said.

"It is cold." I held my hands up to the heat. "It's going to snow soon." I didn't need my phone's weather app to tell me that.

"Hector says if you go now, you can still make your way to Denver," Andrea said. "Before you get snowed in for the winter."

"Is that what Hector said?" I asked, keeping my tone light. "Is he trying to get rid of me?" If he knew that I was staying here without any ability to pay my way, he probably really would.

"Maybe he's just trying to be helpful," Andrea said.

"I appreciate his concern," I said, knowing we weren't talking about Hector anymore. "But if it's all the same to him, I think I would like to stay here."

"Were you out looking for work?" Dakota asked.

At my curious gaze, she shrugged. "I saw you leaving this morning. Before breakfast." She glanced at Andrea. "And well, I just know."

It was clear to me that somehow Dakota knew I didn't have a room. It wouldn't take much for someone to discover me sleeping down here on the couch. Then I would have some serious explaining to do.

I'd been planning on using the cold for an excuse, but since I knew the girls were sleeping upstairs, I couldn't bring myself to claim that I couldn't bear sleep in the cold.

Since I had no reason to hide that particular piece of information about myself I simply told her the truth.

"I was and I found something," I said.

"What kind of work?" Andrea asked.

"I'm going to be working for Dr. Avery," I said.

"What kind of work?" she asked suspiciously.

I almost laughed. The two girls had no idea just how alike they truly were.

"Medicine," I said. "I worked as a medic in the war." It wasn't a lie. I just didn't say which war.

"Impressive," Dakota said to me, then looked over at Andrea. "I think Bailey might be onto something."

"Bailey is most definitely not onto anything," Andrea said, holding her book up to her chin, glaring at her sister.

"What is it Bailey is onto?" I asked.

Now they were both looking at me, not saying a word.

Dakota set her needlepoint aside. "I need to go do something else," she said.

I sat down in the chair she had vacated.

"Looks like it's just you and me," I said, wondering just what kind of sibling thing I had walked right into.

CHAPTER 24
Andrea

"MY SISTERS HAVE ABSOLUTELY no sense whatsoever,"
I said, setting my book aside. As much as I wanted to hide
behind it, it would have been the height of rudeness.

And if I was going to be rude to anyone, it wouldn't be
Reed.

It was not quite midmorning, yet I had been completely
relaxed by the warm fire, almost lulled to sleep by the crackling flames and steady ticking of the grandfather clock. It
was so much warmer down here than it was upstairs anyway.

Hector was baking something that smelled a lot like
blueberry muffins.

I had been more content than I had been in months.

I would have been more content, though, if my sisters
had not gone completely mad.

It seemed that while I was busy deciding which one of
them should be married off first, they had taken it upon

themselves to decide that I needed a husband. And not just any husband, but Reed.

If I were honest with myself, I had to admit that I had brought this on myself. At least a little bit.

I was the one who had sketched Reed's image into my sister's sketchpad, but she should not have been looking. I had hidden the whole pad in my own trunk, after all.

And although I had not thought to ask her what she was doing going through my things, I had every intent on doing so.

"Sisters can be pesky sometimes," Reed said. "I only have one. I can't imagine having three of them."

"You were fortunate," I said. "Especially when they conspire against you."

A smile tugged at Reed's lips. "Want to share what they were conspiring about?"

"You would not believe it if I told you."

"That bad, huh?"

Before I could answer, another of my errant sisters interrupted us.

"I'll tell you," Bailey said, coming into the room. She had a piece of paper rolled up in her hands.

Oh no.

"No. You won't," I said, getting up to take what I absolutely knew was the drawing I had made.

"It's not that bad," Bailey said, ducking behind a chair.

"You're right," I said. "It isn't that bad. And I refuse to play games with you." I sat back down.

Bailey was not going to trick me into looking like a fool in front of Reed.

She stood there, a full minute, waiting to see if I meant it. Or if I was merely waiting for her to let her guard down.

When I picked up my book and wrapped my blanket back around me, she came out from behind the chair and went to stand in front of Reed.

"My sisters and I have an idea," she said, still watching me carefully out of the corner of her eyes.

"Her sisters," I said. "Not mine."

They both looked at me curiously.

"Don't bring me into it," I said. "I have nothing to do with this."

"Well," Bailey said. "It's actually all about you."

I pretended to look at the words on the book. I had several ways I could come out of this and not look completely foolish. I could deny drawing it. Or I could simply admit drawing it. A girl had a right to practice after all.

"Are you going to tell me?" Reed said. "Or is this a guessing game?"

I hid a smile behind my book. Reed was actually quite funny.

And I would never admit it, but I liked him quite a bit.

Even if he was a rake.

CHAPTER 25
Reed

"How many guesses do I get?" I asked.

Whatever Bailey held in her hands—a rolled up piece of paper—held some kind of significance for Andrea.

Andrea was pretending not to be concerned, but she was quite troubled by this whole thing.

And I couldn't help but believe that this had something to do with me, though I wasn't quite sure what.

If I had to guess, it was the drawing she had made. The one she refused to show last night. The one had inadvertently led to me kissing her on the cheek.

I had contemplated quite seriously kissing her on the lips, but I had decided in the moment that I should save that first kiss for a private time. Not one with all her siblings watching.

"I'll give you three," Bailey said.

I scratched my chin. Pretended to consider.

"Is it a proclamation of some sort?" I asked.

"Not really," Bailey said, cutting her eyes toward her sister. "But you aren't all that far off."

"How about... a shopping list of some sort?"

Bailey laughed. "No. But I wouldn't mind. I could use a new dress. Maybe some new boots. You get one more."

"Okay," I said, deciding to put her out of her misery. "Is it the drawing that Andrea made in your sketchbook?"

Bailey obviously thought I had either forgotten or hadn't been paying attention last night.

"It is the drawing," she said. "Would you like to see it?"

I shook my head. "Not until Andrea shows it to me."

"Oh." Bailey seemed at a loss. "I don't think she will."

"Okay," I said, getting up to poke at the logs in the fireplace.

Bailey went to sit next to her sister on the sofa. Andrea tried to push her away with her feet, but Bailey stayed.

"Stop it." I heard Andrea whisper.

"No," Bailey said. "It's a good idea."

"It's not."

Turning, I wiped my hands on my jeans and studied the two girls.

"You do know that the two of you are just making me all the more curious, right?" I asked.

"You should marry Andrea," Bailey blurted.

Andrea pushed her off the sofa with her feet.

Bailey landed on the floor with a thump, but she

promptly got up and handed me the rolled up piece of paper before she went back in the kitchen, leaving us alone again.

I simply handed the paper to Andrea.

"I think this belongs to you," I said.

"Please forgive my sister," I said. "She isn't in her right mind."

I laughed. "She seems sane enough."

"No." Andrea set her book aside again and sat up. "She is certifiably insane. Her and Dakota both."

"They both think you should marry me?"

"Yes. Both of them," she said, her cheeks flushed prettily.

"Why do you think they came up with that idea?"

"Insane," she said.

I ran a hand through my hair. Then along my cheek. "I didn't think I was that bad," I mused. "I probably do need to shave though."

"No," Andrea said quickly. "It's not that."

I grinned at her.

"Oh." She took a breath. Let it out on a huff. "You are such a rake."

She put her feet back on the sofa and opened her book. I don't think she even noticed that it was upside down.

I took heart that she had not stormed off. A good sign, at least, that she did not find me completely revolting.

"I heard that rakes make good husbands," I said. I actually hadn't heard any such thing. I was just making this up as I went. I hardly even knew what a rake was until I met her. Wasn't hard to figure out though.

She looked at me over her book, her eyes wide.

"You've been talking to my sisters," she said, accusingly.

"I have not. I promise."

But while I had her attention and no one else was around, it seemed as good a time as any to tell her.

"I have something to tell you," he said.

CHAPTER 26
Andrea

My heart was just about going to pound right out of my chest.

Reed was sitting right here in front of me talking about, of all things, marriage.

If I didn't die of embarrassment first, I was going to kill my sisters.

The warmth of the fireplace was making my face hot. I shoved my hair back. Lifted it up, then let it fall back down. No. It was not the fire. It was the way Reed was looking at me.

He'd been smiling, but now he was looking at me with the utmost serious expression.

He was most definitely making me nervous.

I heard my sisters talking in the kitchen. Heard Hector laugh. I just hoped they stayed out of my sight and away from Reed for awhile. Forever.

The scent of muffins that had smelled so appetizing earlier was making my stomach queasy.

"What is it?" I asked, crossly. He needed to just tell me and put me out of my misery.

He leaned forward, lowered his voice.

"I'm not from here," he said.

I shook my head in exasperation. "Nobody is *from* here."

"No," he said. "That's not what I meant."

The clock chimed the hour. We sat quietly looking at each other until after the eleventh chime.

"I'm not from this *time.*"

"Ok," I said.

The seconds ticked past, turning into a minute. Maybe two.

"I'm from the future."

"That's not possible," she said, dismissing me, turning her attention to arranging the blanket around her legs.

"That's what I thought," I said. "But turns out it is."

"So why are you here?" she asked.

I sat back. "You don't seem surprised."

"I have four younger siblings," she said. "There's nothing I haven't heard."

I laughed. It wasn't funny, though. It wasn't an amused laugh. It felt more like a desperate laugh.

She looked back up at me. "You're serious," she said.

"I am serious."

"Prove it," she said.

"How am I supposed to prove—?" On a sudden burst of inspiration, I pulled out my cell phone. Placed it in her hand.

"What's this?" she asked.

"It's my cell phone." With absolutely no battery.

"It's a mirror," she handed it back. "You should clean it."

I laughed my desperate laugh again. "Doesn't matter," I said. "That's not the point."

"What is the point?"

"The point is that I would not make a good husband."

"Because you're a rake."

"Because I have nothing to my name."

"So?"

"So I would not be able to take care of you."

"That's not a good reason," she said, gazing at me with her siren green eyes.

I was so very confused now. I couldn't tell if she was trying to convince me that I should marry her or if I shouldn't.

I leaned forward again. "I don't even have a room. I can't pay my way. I have no money."

"It's okay," she said. "I can pay for your room until you start getting paid."

How could she be so unconcerned that I might be from another time? And at the same time unconcerned that I had no job.

I honestly did not think she believed a word I was saying.

CHAPTER 27
Andrea

I DID NOT BELIEVE a word Reed was saying.

Hector brought out a tray of freshly baked muffins and a pitcher of water. Left on the end table. Just like my sisters to start something, then just disappear. Sending poor Hector out to bring us muffins and water.

Hector put one muffin on a little plate. Handed it to me. Then handed one to Reed.

We thanked him and he went back into the kitchen.

Reed took a bite of his muffin. I just sat and held mine. I had no appetite.

Why would he think he could tell me stories like this? Stories about being from another time. About not having anything to offer.

I'd heard about men like him. Men who would offer any excuse to avoid getting married.

But the joke was on him. I did not want to marry him.

No matter what my sisters said.

I took a deep breath. Forced my heart rate to slow down. Decided to turn it around on him.

"Why do you want to marry me?" I asked.

"Why do I—?" He set his plate down. "I never said..."

"Then you don't want to?"

"I don't know. Your sister started it."

I laughed. He was kinda cute when he was baffled and confused.

A log crumbled in the fireplace sending sparks flying. A wagon rumbling along the street outside. Everyone was scurrying to get ready for the snowfall.

"I guess you'll be staying here through the winter," I said.

"I guess I will."

"So tell me, Mr. Smith from the future. Why are you here?"

"I keep asking myself that very question."

"You must have an idea."

"I think maybe it's fate."

I shook my head. "I don't think it's a very good kind of fate."

"Why would you say that?"

"Well. You have no means. Even more, you're a single man in need of a wife with no means." I actually said that with a straight face.

"You're right," he said. "I should have done a better job with choosing my fate."

"You can't choose your—" I stopped myself in midsentence. Reed and I were simply going around and around in circles.

But he wasn't deterred. "I think maybe a person can choose their fate. To an extent."

"Maybe," I said. "But I think that might be an illusion. When I think about all the things that have happened to me. My father going to war. Being killed. My mother dying. All those things happened to get me here. I had nothing to do with it. So maybe it's simply fate. I had nothing to do with those things." My bit my lip to keep it from trembling.

"I'm sorry," he said. "You're right. There are a lot of things we can't control. But I like to think that we do indeed choose things every day and those things add up to send us in one direction or another."

"What do you mean?" I wiped at my eyes. I didn't talk about my parents. My siblings and I just didn't. It was one of those rare tacit agreements that somehow worked for us. Kept us moving forward and not dwelling on the past.

"Well, take you for example. You chose to do the right thing. You chose to keep your family together. To bring them here at the request of your father."

"I suppose."

"And you have choices right now. What you choose to do today determines the general direction of your life."

"Maybe. But it's nearly impossible to change a direction once it starts."

"Like the Titanic," he said.

"The what?"

"Nothing. It's a ship in the future. A really big boat. For it to change directions, they have to start way ahead of time."

"Why would you want to stay in the past?" I asked.

"Maybe I like it here," he said. "Maybe I like you."

CHAPTER 28
Reed

I HAD BEEN ALONE for a long time. A really long time.

I had been alone by choice. Not alone alone. I had what I called companions whenever I wanted, but I didn't have anyone to actually share my life with.

And that had been by choice.

If I had traveled all the way to the past and all evidence suggested that I had, it had to be for a reason.

I don't think something like that could be just happenstance.

And since I *liked* Andrea, I chose to think that maybe I was here to be with her. It was the only thing that made sense to me. Any kind of sense.

I had not seen my name in any of the history books, so I didn't know if I was in some kind of different timeline or if maybe I was just destined to be here.

Didn't matter to me.

What mattered to me was that I right my ship.

I was not a kid. I was retired, for God's sake. Maybe that was messing with my head. I was too young to be retired.

But I was old enough to know that if I wanted to do something I couldn't stop waiting. I was going to run out of time.

It was funny.

When I was young, I didn't understand just how fast things were going to move when I was grown up.

My grandmother used to say that as kids it wasn't that we think we're going to live forever. We just don't understand how fast life goes. When we're looking ahead, we think the years are going to last a lot longer than they do.

But instead, the years are like a freight train. Once they get going, they just speed up. Faster and faster. Then before we know it, we've run all the way to the end.

And unfortunately, it's a one way trip.

So sitting here in 1866 with the girl of my dreams, I decided that putting things off and wasting time was not a good option.

"I like you," I said again with more conviction. "And I think you would make a good wife. I feel a connection with you. I feel like you give me purpose."

There. I'd said what I really thought.

I was done with playing games. That kind of game anyway. I was on board for playing parlor games and board games all day long, but not games that mattered.

Andrea put her feet on the floor, but she just stared into

the flames. I didn't think she was going to say anything. I had overstepped.

"I feel it, too," she said, barely loud enough for me to hear the words.

A slow grin spread across my lips.

This was perhaps going to work out better than I had thought.

I had put all my cards on the table. All or nothing.

But it had paid off.

If she felt what I felt, then we were indeed going to make a perfect couple.

I had never felt such a strong pull toward someone. Not even in grade school when I'd actually had a girlfriend.

No. This was different.

This was Kismet.

I'd stake the career I'd had on it.

CHAPTER 29
Andrea

MY SIBLINGS, all four of them, made their way into the parlor and settled down to do whatever they were doing.

Bailey had her sketchpad out and a charcoal pencil. Dakota was knitting some socks, being practical. Elise settled in with a book. And Colton was at the window messing with a sextant someone—an older widow whose husband had passed—from the wagon train had given him.

But them being here, in effect, put a halt to the conversation Reed and I were having. Bailey, after starting such a fuss about my marrying Reed, was acting like nothing at all had happened.

Of course, she had no way of knowing that I was plotting her demise.

"It's snowing," Colton announced with all the enthusiasm of an adolescent boy.

My sisters all dropped what they were doing and rushed to the window to see.

Reed looked at me. "Want to go outside? Check it out?"

"Let's go out back," I said.

After stopping at the kitchen to bundle up in cloaks and gloves and hats, we stepped outside into the cold of the early afternoon.

I stood at the top of the stairs, watching the fat snowflakes, the first of the season, drifting from the sky.

"It's beautiful," I said, then went down the steps to stand in the falling snow. Turning my face up to it, I let it fall on my face. Snowflakes landing in my hair. My eyelashes. On my lips.

I was enchanted.

Grinning from ear to ear, I twirled around to find Reed standing next to me.

"I've never seen snow before," I said. "At least not that I can remember. It's beautiful."

"It is beautiful," Reed said, but he was watching me.

The way he was looking at me had my heart doing summersaults.

I didn't know what would happen next.

We had declared that we had a connection. That we liked each other.

I had very little, if any, experience in these matters. I had been fifteen years old when the war had started. I had never been courted. And being the oldest of my sisters, I had no one to model after in this area.

I was on my own.

Reed took my gloved hands in his and twirled me around, then pulled me close, almost touching, but not quite. Like a waltz.

When he put a gloved hand on my cheek, my eyes fluttered closed.

He kissed one eyelid, then the other.

"You're beautiful," he said.

My heart was beating dangerously fast and I fisted my hands in my skirt to keep them steady.

Reed's lips were soft and gentle on my eyelids. I yearned to feel them on my lips, but instead he kissed me on the forehead and released me.

I did not even care that he was a rake.

Maybe his roguishness made him all the more attractive. He was charming and a little bit more than dangerous. But yet he liked *me*.

And I liked everything about him.

No matter what happened from here, there was one thing I knew for certain.

My life was never going to be the same again.

CHAPTER 30
Reed

SINCE I WAS SCHEDULED to start work the next day, my worries about not being able to pay my way at the boarding-house diminished significantly.

I even talked Hector into giving me one of the two vacant bedrooms upstairs.

Things were most definitely looking up.

The snow was light and beautiful, on and off the rest of the day. More on than off.

I settled next to Andrea with a book of my own and enjoyed the rest of a pleasant afternoon with her family. They planned parlor games for after supper entertainment.

But after supper, Dr. Avery came calling, interrupting any plans.

The three of us, Dr. Avery, Andrea, and myself went into the kitchen and sat at the table. Dr. Avery slid the letter across the table for Andrea to read.

She slowly unfolded it and laid it out on the table.

"It's not a letter," she said.

"No," Dr. Avery said. "It's not a letter."

She was quiet as she read, then slid it over to me.

"You knew about this?" she asked him.

"I knew about it," he said. "but I didn't know the details."

"Do you know how it happened?" she asked.

"Not really," he said. "I think your father was planning on bringing all of you out here to live after the war."

She nodded.

I finished reading the document and looked up at Andrea. "This house is yours," he said. "It belongs to your family."

"Is it legal?" she asked Dr. Avery.

"It is legal," he said. "I see no reason why it wouldn't be. We'll go into Boulder City in the spring and have the necessary paperwork done. But in the meantime," he said with a little smile. "The boardinghouse is officially closed for business."

Andrea looked at me. "This is our home," she said.

"Congratulations," I said, not knowing what else to say.

Dr. Avery looked at me, then back to Andrea. "There's a stipend attached to the house. I've been using it to pay Hector and expenses. But it's yours to do with whatever you want."

"I definitely want to keep Hector," she said. "Is there enough to hire a housekeeper?" she asked.

"There's enough to do whatever you want." Dr. Avery

looked at me. "Does this change your plan to come to work tomorrow?"

"No," I said. "I don't think so." I looked at Andrea. "Unless you need me to do something."

"Whatever you want to do," she said.

I could tell by the expression on her face that she was still absorbing everything.

"I'll be there," I told Dr. Avery.

And this, I realized was quite simply how it had happened. How Andrea had become one of the influential people during the early days of Whiskey Springs.

There was only one thing that troubled me. In all the books I had looked through, I had seen no mention of her getting married.

Every mention of her had been Andrea Auclair.

CHAPTER 31
Andrea

IT TOOK a few days for us to grasp the full meaning of owning the boardinghouse.

First, it was no longer a boardinghouse. Second, All five of us now had our own bedrooms. It was a luxury I thought we had lost when we'd been forced to leave our home in Natchez.

The sixth bedroom was occupied by Reed. I found it interesting that no one said anything about it. No one asked me if he was paying rent. I think my younger siblings were so removed from responsibility that no one even thought about it.

And I didn't say anything. I liked having him here and, besides, he was gone all day working with Dr. Avery.

In the evenings we played parlor games with Reed fitting right in as though he had always been part of the family.

The snow had backed off and allowed fall to last a little

bit longer, but the evenings were still quite cold by my southern girl standards.

It had been nearly a week since the snowfall and romantic moment Reed and I had shared.

He hadn't brought up the story about being from the future again, but then we hadn't had any time alone either.

On occasion when I caught him watching me, he would just smile and look away.

Besides Hector, we added another member to our staff, a woman in her mid-thirties who was in need of work and agreed to do the housekeeping. She was around during the day, but did not require a room. She had a home of her own with a husband.

Tonight, a Friday night, however, was a change in the routine. Today the six of us were getting ready to attend a musical at the Whiskey Springs saloon.

A traveling troupe was in town and everyone was going. It was odd that they were performing a musical in the saloon, but it was the only space that could accommodate a crowd.

Before the war, our parents had taken us to plays and musicals a few times, so I was quite excited about going tonight.

I put on my best dress, a ballgown in a deep red. The seamstress back in Natchez had called the color dragon's blood. I don't know where she got the name, but it struck my fancy and even though this was only the second time I had worn it, I was in love with the color.

After Dakota and I styled each other's hair, I pulled on

my white gloves that covered my arms all the way up over my elbows. It seemed a little bit strange to put on my best clothes out here. Even stranger that they had survived the trip.

Dakota had gone downstairs before me, so after one last look at myself in the little mirror over my dresser, I took a deep breath and headed downstairs.

I told myself it was silly to be nervous. But this was the first time I had been out to anything since before the war. And the first time I had gone anywhere escorted by a gentleman.

The war had come during the prime years of my life. I was on the verge of being a spinster now, by the standards of the old days.

I didn't feel like a spinster and I did not feel old at twenty-one. I felt rather fashionable in my dress, over a wide hoop skirt that swayed as I walked.

When I reached the top of the stairs, the clock began to chime the hour.

"Come on, Andrea," Elise called up. "We're going to be late."

We were actually an hour early, but I understood her excitement. The saloon was only a ten minute walk, at most.

Halfway down the stairs, I saw Reed standing below, waiting for me. My heart skittered into an erratic staccato.

He was dressed in a formal suit with a long coat and he wore a white cravat tucked into the vest of his three-piece suit.

Perhaps tonight we would have a few minutes to talk. Alone.

He took my hand as I reached the bottom of the stairs. Helped me balance as I reached the floor.

"You look stunningly beautiful," he whispered for my ears only.

My siblings, waiting at the door for us, went ahead now that I was downstairs, just assuming that we would follow.

I rolled my eyes at their back, but it did not matter anyway. Let them go.

On impulse, I took my little handkerchief in the same color as my dress out of my pocket and reached up to tuck it in Reed's pocket, leaving one end peaking out.

"This is an unusual color," he said, looking down at the handkerchief.

"It's called dragon's blood," I said, looking up into his eyes. "They say it has magical qualities."

"Is that so? Well a little magic can be a good thing."

"I think so."

He placed a finger beneath my chin and tilted my head up just a little while he lowered his head.

His lips pressed against mine with a feathery soft touch. I leaned in, wanting more, and we stood that way, absorbing the feel of each other as the clock ticked off a handful of seconds.

Then we both straightened.

With a little smile, I tucked my hand in the crook of his arm and together we walked toward the door.

Since my siblings had gone out ahead of us, we were last to go out.

Reed held the door as I stepped out and he followed.

Feeling his arm slipping from mine, I stopped.

My hand slid along his arm, until our hands were touching. He grasped at my hand. I felt it ever so faintly as I turned, looking over my shoulder.

He looked at me. An expression of alarm on his face.

Then his hand slipped out of mine and he was gone.

Just like that.

Reed was gone.

CHAPTER 32
Reed

I STOOD ON THE SIDEWALK. In the dark. A traffic light, set to nighttime caution mode, blinked off to my left.

It was late. Very late. Or very early. Depending on a person's perspective. Either way, I was the only person on the street.

I stood perfectly still as a car, a little modern sports car with music blaring, zipped by.

Then it was quiet again. Rock music coming from the bar next door registered somewhere in my brain.

The only thought that stood out clearly in my head was that I was not in 1866 anymore. That thought was accompanied by an image of Andrea.

My hand slipping from hers as she turned. The look of shock on her face.

I could still feel her warm lips on mine.

Looking down, I saw that I was still wearing the suit Dr. Avery had loaned me.

I pulled the little square of silk out of my breast pocket.

Dragon's blood.

Such an odd name for a color. It was actually a hauntingly beautiful deep red.

I pressed the cloth to my lips. It smelled like Andrea. Like honeysuckle and jasmine.

Standing there on the street, I gave my thoughts a chance to settle.

I had done the thing that I knew better than to do. The thing that I had not done since the last time I had gone back in time.

I had gone out the front door.

Making sure to avoid it, I'd been using the back door.

But I'd gotten comfortable. And I guess I thought that as long as I was holding Andrea's hand, I would be okay.

But the door was the portal. It was the only answer.

And I had just walked right through it. Like I had good sense.

Which I was obviously sorely lacking.

I turned around abruptly, bumping into the closed door right behind me. I turned the knob. Hard. Pressed my shoulder against the door. Turned the knob again.

Then I slammed my fist against the ungiving wood and pressed my forehead against it.

I'd had everything going right.

I had a job. A place to live.

And I had Andrea.

I had decided that I was going to ask her to marry me. I was just waiting for the right time. Saving up my money for a ring.

But then I'd walked through the front door. Like an idiot. I'd walked right out of the world I wanted to be in, leaving the girl I wanted to be with.

"Back at it again?" Officer Garrison asked, coming up behind me.

I slowly straightened and took a deep breath. The last thing I felt like doing right now was talking to anyone, much less explaining why I was standing at the door to a condemned building.

"Just taking a break," I said.

"Nice costume."

"Yeah," I looked down at the suit I had been so proud to be wearing. And now it just looked out of place.

It looked like I felt.

"Look man," Officer Garrison said. "I don't know what you've got going on, but can I give you some advice?"

"Sure," I said, certain I wasn't going to get away from him without hearing what he had to say.

"Just go home," he advised. "Wherever home is. Not your cabin, but go home."

"I don't have a home," I said.

"Good Lord, Man," he said. "That's your problem. Pull yourself together. Get an apartment somewhere. You need a place to call home."

"I had a place to call home," I said, feeling like I was going to break into a thousand pieces.

"At least go to your cabin. Sleep it off. Things will look better in the morning."

I looked at Officer Garrison. "You're right," I said. "Things usually look better in the morning." And I needed some sleep. Tomorrow I would figure out what I needed to do. Figure out how I was going to get back to Andrea.

And get back to her I would. Even if I had to tear this place apart piece by piece. I was going back.

If it was the last thing I did.

CHAPTER 33
Andrea

REED WAS GONE.

I dropped to my knees.

Oh God. I tried to catch my breath.

Dakota must have looked back over her shoulder. Saw me there.

I lowered my head to the floor, my skirts billowing out around me.

"What's happened?" Dakota asked, running up to kneel beside me. "Are you hurt?"

"No. I'm not hurt," I shook my head. I'm shattered.

"Where is Reed?" Colton asked.

"He's gone." The words were barely a whisper. I couldn't catch my breath.

"Where did he go?"

They were all talking at once. I gave up on answering anyone and just knelt there with my head down.

"Get her some water," Bailey said, but since no one could get past me through the door, Bailey cupped her mouth with her hands and called Hector's name.

"What's happened?" Hector asked, coming running.

"I don't know. Will you bring her a glass of water?"

"Do we have any smelling salts?"

"I don't need smelling salts," I said, sitting up. "I just need a minute." I swiped at them with my hands. "Just give me some space."

Hector was back in a minute with a glass of water.

"Where is Mister Reed?" he asked.

"He's not in the house with you?" Colton asked.

"I told you, he's gone," I said, trying to keep my voice steady. Pretty sure I wasn't doing a good job with that.

"People don't just disappear," Bailey said, standing over me, her hands on her hips.

I looked at her, focusing on my sister's face. "When did you become the expert?"

It was such a bizarre question, it kept them all quiet for about five seconds.

"We need to get her inside," Colton said. "Come." He gently took my arm. "Let's get you inside so we can figure out what's happened."

I allowed Colton to help me stand since I couldn't stay there on the front porch forever. He guided me to the sofa then handed me the glass of water.

I heard my sisters talking in the background. For some reason, they didn't seem to think I could hear them. Or didn't care.

"Maybe she's gone insane."

"Where is Reed?"

"He's the only one who can comfort her."

"She said he left."

"Where would he go?"

"Have you seen Reed at all?"

"I last saw him standing with Andrea," Hector said.

I looked over at Hector, wondering just how much he had seen.

Had he seen me kissing Reed?

I drank some more water, then closed my eyes.

I didn't even care. I could still feel Reed's lips on mine.

Reed was the love of my life. The one I wanted to spend the rest of my life with.

But I'd done the worst thing a person could do to the one they loved.

I hadn't believed him.

He really was from the future.

CHAPTER 34
Reed

I STAYED in my cabin for three days.

I barely ate anything. I slept more than I had ever slept at the time.

Maybe it was from the time travel. Or maybe it was from the broken heart.

Or maybe it was both.

Whatever it was, I was absolutely shattered.

I'd seen the movies. I knew how hard it was to get back to someone after leaving them in another time period. Richard never got back to Elise.

Finally, after three days, I got up to find something to eat.

I was not going to be deterred. I was going to do whatever I needed to do to go back to her.

My bread was molded. My milk was curdled. I had nothing to eat. I took the trash can and swept all the food I'd bought when I first got here into the trash, tied it up, and took it outside to the metal bear protected can.

I took a shower, standing beneath the hot water until it ran cold.

I felt like I was moving under water. In slow motion.

After my shower, I put on some clean clothes. I'd left my boots back in 1866, so I put on my canvas sneakers.

Leaving the cabin, I stopped at the first restaurant I came to. A little pizza parlor that I had never even been in.

I sat off to myself and ordered a cheese pizza. Forced myself to eat half of it.

Not wanting to interact with anyone, I left twice as much cash on the table as I need to and kept walking.

With no direction in mind, I found myself at the library.

Looked like they were still open.

It didn't take me long to find the same books I had looked through what seemed like a lifetime ago.

And it didn't take me any time at all to see that I had altered history.

In all the places I had seen Andrea's name, I saw Bailey's name instead. And Colton's

I glared at the offending books. What, then, had happened to Andrea? It was like she never existed.

That could not be right. *I* was the one who had gone through time. She was still there. She had not come with me. Now if she had, that would have solved all sorts of problems.

Except that she belonged there. In 1866. She had means and a family.

But now she had quite simply vanished from the history books.

I turned the page in one of the older of the books, the fragile page crinkling beneath my fingers. To the photo of her family. They were all there. Bailey, Colton, Dakota, and Elise. But Andrea wasn't there.

Sitting back, I pressed a hand against my brow.

What had happened?

Had I transmitted some disease to her? Had I killed her?

Not giving up, I kept looking. Surely there was at least a note somewhere. Something about there being five Auclair siblings who had come to Whiskey Springs in 1866.

But despite my determination to find something, I came up empty handed.

One of the librarians came to my table. Reminded me that the library was closing.

So now I was closing down libraries. My buddies would have loved giving me hell about this.

"Are there any other records?" I asked the librarian. "about the early days of Whiskey Springs?"

"That's all I know about," she said. "I'm sorry. What kind of research are you doing?"

What kind of research indeed? "Just working on my family history," I said.

"You know," she asked. "about the legend?"

"What legend?"

"According to the legend, Whiskey Springs has always had a magical quality to it. At least in the early years. It was a place where people who had lost touch would magically find each other."

The librarian, Mary, according to her name tag, looked directly at me. "Are you looking for someone, Reed?"

"I—," I didn't remember telling Mary my name. I hadn't told anyone here at the library my name. I was certain of it. I hadn't checked anything out, so I hadn't needed to.

Mary smiled warmly at me. Patient. That was the best word to describe her. As though she had nowhere else she would rather be or needed to be.

"Maybe," I said.

"I'm going to tell you a secret," she said, dropping gracefully into the chair next to mine. "My name isn't really Mary."

I went on alert. Glancing around. But it looked like we were the only ones left in the library.

"My name is Vaughn Becquerel."

"Vaughn." Vaughn had been the name of grandmother's grandmother. The one who had come over from France and traveled through time.

"You know my name, yes?" she asked.

"I've heard it." My throat was dry. I studied this woman's face. Hoping to find something familiar.

"I was born in France in the 1700s."

I swallowed and let her words sink in. "You're my great-great-great-great grandmother?"

"Something like that," she said. "I lose count. When I try to figure it out, it makes me feel old."

"How are you here?"

"Over time my time traveling has become focused on helping those who need my help."

"I need your help?" I asked.

"That depends," she said. "How much do you love Andrea?"

I sucked in a breath. Forced myself to stay steady. Mary. Vaughn. This woman knew about Andrea. That told me she was legitimate. "I love her enough to give up everything to be with her. And if I can't find my way back to her, I'm not sure my life will have purpose."

She nodded slowly.

"Good," she said. "This is good."

"It doesn't feel so good right now."

She put a hand on my shoulder.

"Have faith," she said, smiling warmly at me again. "I can help you."

CHAPTER 35
Andrea

"ARE you sure you want to do this?" Dakota asked for the umpteenth time.

I steadied myself as the horse shifted beneath me.

In front of the Whiskey Springs stables, I sat astride a horse I had bought from a fellow named Brantley Jackson. The mare's name was Sprite and aptly named, she had a bit of spirit in her.

I wore my fur lined cloak over my one riding habit. I had on warm gloves and a warm hat that I had bought at the General Store. Yet still, I was cold.

Snow clouds had gathered around the mountain peaks. The snow, when it came, was going to be beautiful, but I would have to see it from afar.

With Dakota's help, I had packed everything I needed into two saddlebags.

I could not stay here without Reed.

I had left everything my sisters would need, all the paperwork, taking only what I needed for myself.

Dakota was the only one I had told.

I was leaving Whiskey Springs. I would go into Denver. Find a little cottage. Make a life for myself.

Start over without the memory of Reed at every turn.

If I stayed here, I would spend all my time watching for him. I knew this. It was how I had spent the last two weeks.

"It's going to snow," Dakota said.

"I'll be down the mountain before that. "Besides I have my guide."

Dakota glanced over at the burly mountain man I had hired to escort me to Denver. Dr. Avery had vouched for the fellow. Claimed the man had escorted his own wife. So I felt safe.

"I don't want you to go," she said.

"I know. But I'll write you. I'll be less than three hours away, so we can visit."

"There's nothing that can change your mind?" she asked.

There was one thing, but the odds were stacked against it.

Reed had merely been a time visitor. Now he had gone on his way. It had broken my heart, but I had accepted it.

"You'll be fine," I said. "Everything is set up for all of you to be taken care of."

"It won't be the same," Dakota said, her eyes moist.

I looked away. If I hesitated much longer, my resolve would crumble. I had to do this. I had to do it for me.

"Goodbye Dakota," I said and nudged the horse forward.

The guide followed at a respectable distance.

I spurred the horse into a trot. The cold wind stung my exposed face.

But I preferred the sting of the cold to the pain in my heart.

I had made my decision and there was no turning back. The mare, Sprite, easily found her footing on the rocky trail that led down the mountain.

After the path circled to the right and Whiskey Springs was no longer visible to me, I slowed down.

Let the pain wash over me.

It will pass. If I repeated that to myself enough, it would be true. Right?

I let my mind go blank as Sprite made her way along the trail headed toward Denver.

I needed to look forward. Not backwards.

With the roar of the river off to my right, I forced myself enjoy the splendor of the countryside. It was so very beautiful.

Maybe I would come back here later. After my heart had had time to heal.

Right now, I just needed to get away.

I glanced over my shoulder. The guide was merely a few feet behind me.

But...

I pulled on Sprite's reins, bringing the horse to a stop. Then I looked again.

There was another rider approaching behind the guide.

I had made Dakota promise not to tell anyone I was leaving. I had left a note for my siblings. No one else knew.

Maybe it was just someone else on the trail. Someone else trying to beat the snowfall. I nudged Sprite aside. The rider could just go on past.

I pulled the hood of my cloak over my head and turned away so I wouldn't be required to engage in meaningless conversation. Or worse have someone want to travel along with us.

The rider approached. Conversed briefly with the guide. A male. Of course. Only a male would be out riding this trail alone.

I leaned forward, running a hand along Sprite's neck.

The rider was beside me now.

He stopped.

With a resigned sigh, I straightened and turned to greet the rider.

The wind caught my hood and tossed it back.

My heart lodged itself in my throat.

The rider was Reed.

CHAPTER 36
Reed

IT WAS A COLD DAY. Too cold to be riding.

It was going to be snowing in no time. Already, the clouds were gathering around the mountain peaks.

Squirrels skittered about in the fallen leaves, gathering their nuts for the winter.

The scent of the fir and spruce trees was pleasantly strong along the burbling river.

Andrea had not been at the boarding house when I arrived. But her sister, Dakota had quickly given her up.

Andrea had decided to pack her bags and leave. That, at least, explained why all records of her had been erased from Whiskey Springs's history.

And now I knew that time lines could be altered.

I had not been in the original history books because I had not been there yet.

Andrea looked at me with disbelief. Like I was a ghost.

Her face was flushed from the cold. The hood had fallen back and her hair fell softly around her face.

"Reed."

"Hello Love."

Then she smiled and my heart burst with joy.

I slid off my horse, then helped her slide off hers.

I gathered her into my arms and hugged her as close as I could.

Our hearts, seeming to beat as one, were the only thing I could hear over the roaring of the river as the water rushed over the rocks.

Then I pulled back and searched her siren green eyes.

"I understand we're moving to Denver," I said.

"I needed to get away," she said, biting her lip.

"Agreed," I said. "The farther away from the boarding-house door we are, the better."

"What happened?" she asked.

"The door is a portal through time," I said. "For me, at least."

She searched my eyes. "Then let's stay as far away from that particular door as we can," she said.

"You're the perfect woman for me," I said.

"Miss," the guide called. "Would like me to stay? Or should I go?"

"Does that mean you can stay?" she asked me.

"That's the plan," I said. "If you'll have me, wild horses couldn't pull me away."

"You can go," she told the guide.

The guide galloped off, leaving us alone.

And standing here with the cool breeze swirling around us, I had absolutely no doubt that I was in the place I wanted to be.

I was in the time I wanted to be.

As long as I was with Andrea, nothing else mattered.

 Epilogue
ANDREA

DENVER in the winter was like a winter wonderland.

The mountains in the distance were capped with snow and oftentimes hidden in a blanket of clouds.

Whenever the clouds cleared, there was even more snow than before.

And today it was snowing in Denver. The soft flat flakes drifted like confetti, covering everything.

I stood at the window of my upstairs sitting room—with a fireplace to keep me warm—and looked out over the street below.

Horses and carriages hustled and bustled this way and that. Especially today. Christmas Eve.

Everyone had someplace to go.

And tonight Reed and I had someplace to go.

I had on my favorite dress, the one in dragon's blood red, and waited for Reed to escort me downstairs.

Tonight we were going to a play.

We went to something—a play or a symphony—nearly every week. One of the benefits of living in a city, wild and untamed as it might be.

If I overlooked the wildness of it, it actually reminded a great deal of Natchez.

Reed came from our bedroom. "Ready?" he asked.

I whirled around with a ready smile on my lips.

Seeing my husband, Reed Smith, always brought a smile to my lips. It didn't matter whether it was three hours since I had seen him or just three minutes.

The dragon's blood handkerchief was tucked in his breast pocket. He wore it everywhere we went.

In fact, I think he kept it in his pocket all the time.

Perhaps the color had carried a little bit of magic since he'd had it with him when he came back to me, this time to stay.

"You look beautiful," he said, taking me in his arms. "As always."

"So do you."

He kissed me on the tip of my nose. "I have a Christmas present for you."

"What kind of Christmas present?"

He reached into his pocket and pulled out a little box with a white bow tied around it.

"What is it?" I asked.

"You have to open it."

I untied the ribbon, and with a quick glance at his smiling face, I opened the box.

A ring lay nestled on a bed of velvet.

"It's made of dragon's blood," he said, picking it up and sliding it on my finger.

"Dragon blood isn't supposed to be real," I said, examining the fiery red stone band. I looked back up at him. "But maybe it is."

"It's actually a mineral called calcite," he said. "But as far as we're concerned, it's dragon's blood."

"I love it," I said, stretching up to kiss him.

"It's handmade, one of a kind," he said.

"I have a present for you, too."

"You're the only present I need."

"Maybe," I said, impishly. "But this is one of a kind, also."

"Oh?"

I ran a hand along my stomach. "We're going to have a baby."

"A baby?"

I nodded, biting my lip again.

He picked me up and twirled me around in a circle.

I was laughing and trying to catch my breath when he set me back on my feet.

"Your present is by far the best anyone has ever given me. Or ever will."

"We sort of made it together," I said.

"Yes," he said, kissing me again. "we did make it together. That's what makes it so special."

"It's magical," I said.

And indeed, everything about my life was magical.
From Reed, to the baby we had magically made together.

Keep Reading for a preview of Lavender Blue...

KATHRYN KALEIGH

LAVENDER
BLUE

THE BECQUERELS

Lavender Blue

PREVIEW

Chapter 1
Graham Daniels

I STEPPED OUTSIDE onto the front porch of my little log cabin and surveyed my land.

Today was a beautiful springtime day. Nice and cool this morning with a promise of showers in the afternoon, like every afternoon. A warm afternoon followed by a chilly night.

A burbling river ran behind the cabin, making its way over huge boulders creating a rush of water that lulled me to sleep at night. Fragrant spruce and fir trees scattered around the house was home to chipmunks and birds.

I lived side by side in perfect harmony with all animals. Elk. Bears. Big horn sheep.

A two-lane blacktop road ran about twenty yards from

my front porch. From about seven o'clock in the morning to about eight o'clock at night, it was alive with cars and buses carrying hikers and tourists and photographers out to get an up close look at the splendor of the Rocky Mountain National Park.

Across the road, across the meadow, stood the mountains. From here I could see Long's Peak. Always identifiable by the way the rocks resembled a giant beaver climbing up the side of the peak.

Okay. Not technically my land, but it was my job to oversee it.

One of five other full-time National Park rangers, I was the only one who wanted to actually live inside the park. Besides, Maggie, but she didn't count. She'd been here forever. When my predecessor retired, this cabin came up for grabs.

I considered myself most fortunate that no one higher in seniority than me wanted it.

It was perfect. I could live without nosy neighbors. No television. No cell phone service. Just me and nature.

Of course, I had work. That meant I had to routinely lead nature walks. Hikes. Campfire programs. Those didn't bother me. I didn't mind getting out and doing things. I wasn't a recluse. I just preferred to spend my time off alone.

But today was going to be an easy day. Today I had no assignments. On days like this I was allowed to just walk whatever trail I wanted to walk. Explore. Make sure there were no problems. Wear my uniform and answer questions.

Since it was only my third day on the job, I decided I

would hike up to Bierstadt Lake. Check out the trail. See if any maintenance was needed. Since it was one of the trails assigned to me, it seemed like a good one to start off with. Well-traveled. Well loved. An easy hike.

I made myself a latte. A graduation present from myself to myself. It would take a while to get the city out of me. In the meantime, I gave myself a few small pleasures and lattes happened to be one of them.

Took my latte out on the back porch and sat on the one big wooden chair that had come with the place.

I watched the river racing over the rocks. It didn't know it was racing ahead to a waterfall about a mile from here.

Sort of like life, I mused. We raced headlong forward, not having a clue what we were racing toward. *Can't wait for the weekend to get here. Be so glad when this semester is over.* So many people never even lived to see that weekend or the end of that semester. If they knew, perhaps they would slow down, enjoy the day they were in. But instead, we all just raced blindly along toward our waterfalls.

I filled my backpack with bottles of water, granola bars, my park issued satellite phone.

I packed three extra small bottles of water in case I happened across a dehydrated tourist or two.

Added in a notepad and a camera. This was work and I took it seriously.

Just because I happened to love what I did, didn't make me any less responsible. On the contrary.

I took my park ranger truck to the Bear Lake trailhead

and parked at the far end of the parking lot. Didn't want to take up a spot someone else might need. If it hadn't been so far from my cabin, I would have just walked.

I took the trail around Bear Lake first. The most popular hike in the park, it was well maintained with little wooden bridges that made perfect photo backgrounds. Everything seemed to be in order. It was early yet, so not too many tourists. The ranger manning the information booth wasn't even here yet.

After the quick hike around Bear Lake, I veered off onto the Bierstadt Lake trail. The first part of the trail was straight up. I was in good shape, but my breath coming in a bit labored reminded me to take it easy since I hadn't had time to adapt to the elevation yet.

I kept my jacket zipped as I headed up the trail. Even with the change in elevation, it was cooler the higher I went.

I moved quickly over the rocky trail, enjoying the aloneness.

I was in a unique position that I tried not to think about.

It was coming up on the one-year anniversary.

Reaching an area where the park engineers had put bridges on the trail for people to walk on, it looked like I was walking over mist.

I stopped. Grabbed my camera out of the side pocket of my backpack and took a couple of photos. It was beautiful here. There was always a new way to see things and the weather had so much to do with those changes.

The trail leveled off as I neared the lake. I took a couple of notes. Things that could be better. A loose handrail on one of the bridges. A broken step.

When I reached the banks of the lake, I sat on a boulder at the edge of the water and ate a granola bar.

I was the only person here, but I was certain that would change before long.

Mist hovered over the lake, giving it a magical look.

I remembered this lake from when I was a teen. This was one of the good memories. It was odd how the bad memories made the good memories sad. It was like a misery loves company thing.

But I fought it. I fought against those bad memories, doing my best to keep the bad from tainting the good.

It was hard. I readily admitted that to myself.

The light shifted and the mist vanished from the lake.

Sunlight glinted off the water, blinding me for a second.

Deciding to take a walk around the lake, I stashed my water bottle and wrapper in my backpack and left my boulder. But I decided to take a photo first. As a park ranger, I never knew when I might need pictures. My favorite professor had been old-school. He had taught me that.

I hiked toward the right, quickly reaching an open area on the west side of the lake.

My feet froze to the ground.

I saw a beautiful young lady with long brunette hair falling loosely around her shoulders, barely held back by a loosely tied bow.

She wore a long light blue dress with long sleeves and a

high neck. A long dress. As in it billowed out around her where she sat on the ground.

She didn't see me. Her focus was intent on the canvas in front of her. The paint canvas was propped on a little stand and she held a palette of colors in her right hand while she splashed paint onto the canvas with her left.

I looked away. Across the lake. Squeezed my eyes tightly closed.

This was... unexpected. I thought the visions had stopped. It had been a long time since it had happened. And not like this.

I looked back. The girl was still there. I could see her profile now. She was quite lovely. Beautiful actually.

I stared at her longer than I should have. Longer than would have been polite if she was a real person. Longer than I should entertain a vision.

My therapist had taught me better.

Not wanting to look away, but dutifully doing it anyway, I turned around this time. Counted to ten. Then counted to ten again.

The girl should be gone now.

I turned back. Looked in the direction where the girl had been.

Had been.

She was gone now.

But I did not want her to be gone.

I did not want her to be one of my visions.

.   .   .

Chapter 2
Bailey Auclair

1867

I'd had to slip off in the early morning to get some time alone.

Not that I particularly wanted to be alone. I just needed alone time to get any painting done.

It made me a bit cross to have to literally get up with the chickens in order to get that alone time.

But Charlie Jackson followed me around like a puppy. Then there was Drake Lafleur. Drake was a bit older and didn't like me going off without a chaperone. Somehow he seemed to think he was exempt and it was okay for me to go off with him. Like he was my chaperone.

And there was Thomas Beaumont.

I put all three of them out of my mind and focused on getting the hues of the water just right. The reflection of the sun was magical right now. But in just a few minutes, the angle of the sun would change and the hues would be completely different.

Something behind me caught my attention.

I hadn't told anyone I was coming up here, but everyone knew it was my favorite place to come and paint when the weather was right.

It was only a fifteen-minute walk from my back door, so it wasn't far. I didn't see any danger in it. Besides, I knew how to protect myself.

I saw the silhouette of a man off to my left.

"What is it Charlie?" I asked, turning to look over my shoulder.

There was no one there.

Great. Now I was imagining things.

And I was missing the shades of sunlight on the water.

Feeling cross, I dipped my brush into a darker blue and blended it onto the paint already on my canvas.

Deciding that the shade I had just created worked better for the sky, I moved my attention there. The morning sunlight on the misty clouds were pretty, but I quickly did what I did. I changed up what I saw to make it look better on the canvas. Put my own spin on what I was seeing.

And pretty soon I was mixing all sorts of blues together.

I decided I would call this one Lavender Blue.

I saw the man out of the corner of my eyes again. I sat very still. He was a tall, lean man. Wearing some sort of uniform with an odd round hat. His hair was short and he was clean-shaven.

He wasn't Charlie or Drake or Thomas. He wasn't my brother either.

I set my paint brush down very slowly and turned quickly.

But the second I turned, the man vanished.

What the—?

Deciding I had done enough painting for one day—perhaps too many paint fumes—I gathered everything up. Packed in my shoulder bag. I didn't like it that my hands were trembling.

My sister, Andrea, was married to a man who had appeared out of nowhere, then vanished before coming back to stay. She never talked about it, but she didn't have to. I knew.

I knew more than people gave me credit for. I'd learned a long time ago that a smile and a carefully timed blink of the eyes could get me pretty much anything I wanted.

For example, Thomas had agreed to ride into Boulder City to pick up a bolt of material I had ordered for a new dress. I could have it sent here, but that would add on an additional week and I wanted to get it to the seamstress so she could have it ready before the dance next weekend.

There were definitely perks to knowing how to use a smile and a gaze. It wasn't my fault that all girls didn't know how to do that.

I was trying to teach my little sister, Elise, but she was kind of goofy and just ended up giggling. She didn't care about boys. At least not yet. She was still young.

I walked quickly as I followed the little dirt trail home.

I felt unsettled. I'd felt like I was being watched which in itself didn't bother me so much, but having that feeling when there was no one there was the definition of insanity.

I might be a free-spirited artist and all that, but I did not consider myself to be insane.

"What's wrong with you?" Dakota asked when I came in through the back door and went into the parlor.

"Nothing," I said.

Dakota narrowed her eyes at me. "Doesn't look like nothing," she said.

Dakota was the complete opposite of my younger sister Elise. Dakota was suspicious of everyone and nothing got past her.

If something was going on, Dakota would know it.

"The sunlight was wrong," I lied. It had actually been a beautiful morning.

Dakota glanced out the window. "Looks like a perfect day for painting."

I huffed out a breath.

"I got spooked. Okay?"

"Animal?"

"I don't know." I dropped onto the sofa, setting my bag down at my feet and propping my still slightly wet painting next to it. "Where's everybody?" I asked, decided that distraction was my best defense.

"Elise is upstairs napping and Colton is out doing whatever Colton does."

"Right. Any letters?"

She knew I was asking if we had gotten a letter from our oldest sister Andrea who lived in Denver.

"No letters," she said. "Maybe you'll tell me later what happened out there." She picked up her book and opened it.

"Good." I crossed my arms and sat back.

Hector, our small, older Chinese butler brought me tray with a pitcher of water and some little cubes of fresh cheese.

I thanked him and filled a glass with water. Glanced over at Dakota.

I hadn't wanted to talk about what I had seen out there,

but now that I was home and settled, I kind of did. I'd never been one to keep things to myself for very long.

Dakota caught me staring at her and set her book aside. "I thought Thomas was going with you," she said.

"I told him I changed my mind about going. I wanted some alone time to actually paint." Besides, Thomas was handsy. I had no trouble deflecting him. But it took all my attention, making painting next to impossible.

"Can I see it?" she asked.

Dakota and I had never been particularly close. Dakota and Andrea had always been the close ones, but now that Andrea lived in Denver, Dakota was more affable toward her other siblings.

"Of course." I lifted the painting and held it up by the edges. "I'm calling it Lavender Blue," I said.

"When did you start naming your paintings?" she asked.

"All the great artists name their paintings. It's a thing."

"I've never heard of a great artist who paints a new one every day."

"Well. Now you have," I said, feigning offense. Actually, I was pleased that she noticed I finished a painting at least every other day. "I can't help it if I'm prolific."

"I think they're great because they aren't prolific. If everyone had an original, how could they be valuable?"

I just stared at Dakota. She had surely lost her mind. Maybe she just didn't understand.

"Besides, won't you run out of names?" she asked.

"That's silly. I'll never run out of names." I popped a cube of cheese into my mouth. But now she had me thinking. What if I was painting too much? Maybe I'd switch to charcoals for awhile.

"I don't see anything that looks spooky about your painting," she said, circling back around to why I had looked startled when I got home.

"It's nothing you can see, Silly," I said.

Maybe I wouldn't talk about it after all.

Keep Reading Lavender Blue...

(WHEN HEARTSTRINGS ECHO)

Messages Across Time

Falling Through to Forever

Once Upon a Winter's Spell

(BECKONED)

Before the Storm

Twist of Fate

When the Stars Align

Once Upon a Christmas

Once in a Blue Moon

A Wish Upon a Star

(BEGUILED)

When Lightning Strikes

Storm of Time

Midnight Storm

When the Moon Falls

Stormborn Angel

(SPELLED)

Time Tempest

The Heart Remembers

A Moment in Time

Moonlight Shadows

CONTEMPORARY

The Gravity of Us Series
(Reading Order)

Just Breathe

Just Surface

Just Melt

Standalone Suspense

Out of Ashes

Alpine Falls (Maybe Yours) Series
(Reading Order)

Still Yours (Maybe)

Yours for Christmas (Maybe)

Forever Yours (Maybe)

(ALPINE FALLS)

Stranded in Alpine Falls

Belonging in Alpine Falls

The Spirit of Christmas in Alpine Falls

Christmas Wishes in Alpine Falls

Finding True North in Alpine Falls

A Ghost of Christmas Magic in Alpine Falls

Secrets and Second Chances

Honeymoon with a Stranger

Not Our Wedding

(SILVER PINES)

The Way Back to You

Back to Where We Began

When We Were Us

(ONCE UPON FOREVER)

My Forever Guy

Our Forever Love

Forever Vows

Finding Forever

Accidentally Forever

(TRUE NORTH)

Borrowed Until Monday

Still Mine

The Moon and the Stars at Christmas

Perfectly Mismatched

On the Way to Forever

A Merry Little Christmas

On the Way Home to Christmas

It was Always You

(UNBREAK MY HEART)

Begin Again

Love Again

Falling Again

(FOR THE LOVE OF THE FLIGHT)

Just Stay

Just Chance

Just Believe

Just Us

Just Once

Just Happened

Just Maybe

Just Pretend

Just Because

(MAGNETIC NORTH)

Second Chance Kisses

Second Chance Secrets

First Time Charm

Three Broken Rules

Second Chance Destiny

Unexpected Vows

(FALLING FOR CHRISTMAS)

The Heart of Christmas

The Magic of Christmas

In a One Horse Open Sleigh

A Secret Royal Christmas

An Old Fashioned Christmas

(CITY SKYLINE BILLIONAIRES)

Billionaire's Unexpected Landing

Billionaire's Accidental Girlfriend

Billionaire's Fallen Angel

Billionaire's Secret Crush

Billionaire's Barefoot Bride

(TRULY, MADLY, DEEPLY)

The Lady in the Red Dress

On the Edge of Chance

Sealed with a Kiss

Kiss Me at Midnight

The Heart Knows

(STOLEN ECHOES)

When Cupid's Arrow Strikes

Chasing Fireflies

A Chance Encounter

(EDGE OF THE HORIZON)

The Forever Equation

Pretend Boyfriend

All our Tomorrows

Kissing for Keeps

Out of the Blue

The Princess and the Playboy

(RED LIPSTICK KISSES)

Red Lipstick Kisses and Small Town Wishes

Stolen Dances and Big City Chances

Chance Connections and Upside Down Plans

A Christmas Kiss on the Twenty-Fifth

Believe in the Magic of Christmas

Vows of Inheritance Series

(Reading Order)

Vow to Protect

Vow to Redeem

ROMANTASY

(IN THE SPIRIT OF LOVE)

Spirits of the Heart

Out of Dreams and Ashes

Etched Upon the Heart

WESTERN ROMANCE

(LONE STAR HEARTS)

Wanted by a Texas Ranger

Saved by a Texas Ranger

(WHISKEY SPRINGS)

Finding Natalie

Promising Samantha

Falling for Allyson

Saving Savannah

Claiming Charlie

Rescuing Keira

Protecting Gabriella

Courting Isabella

HISTORICAL

(TAPESTRY OF BLUE AND GRAY)

Shadows Beneath Magnolia Blooms

Secrets Among Southern Roses

(IT HAPPENED BY ACCIDENT)

Accidentally Alluring

Accidentally Married

(SOUTHERN BELLE CIVIL WAR)

Beyond Enemy Lines

Love Always

Hearts Under Siege

Hearts Under Fire

Away Down South in Dixie

The Reluctant Bride

Stay with Me

Jasmine Kisses

Magnolia Kisses

Gardenia Kisses

(THE QUINNS)

Wait for Me

Take Me Home

Keep Me Safe

FATED MATES

Riley's Mate

Aiden's Mate

Brayden's Mate

STANDALONE SUSPENSE

Lost and Found

All I Want for Christmas

Serenity

Courting Alley Cat

All of the books in each Series are standalone and can be read out of order. However, some books have characters from the previous stories in them.

www.ingramcontent.com/pod-product-compliance
Lightning Source LLC
Chambersburg PA
CBHW020622110726
47899CB00002B/607